THE BURGLAR WHO STUDIED SPINOZA

Lord, what a feeling!

I'm grateful there isn't something even more despicable than burglary that gives me that feeling, because I probably wouldn't be able to resist it. Oh, I'm a pro, all right, and I do it for the money, but let's not kid ourselves. I draw such an intense charge out of it, it's a wonder lamps don't dim all over the city when I let myself into somebody else's abode.

I don't like criminals. I don't like being one myself.

But I love to steal.

Just suppose.

Just suppose Herbert and Wanda Colcannon are off in Pennsylvania seeing to the breeding of their prizewinning attack dog. And suppose you're the very buttoned-down burglar quoted above, and there's nothing you'd rather steal then Herb's coin collection. And suppose Carolyn Kaiser, your best friend and occasional henchperson and all-time favorite poodle groomer, has all manner of useful information of the Colcannons' schedule.

If you're Bernie Rhodenbarr, I've got news for you. Good news and bad news.

The good news is that the Colcannon carriage house is a setup for burglars, and the bad news is you're not the first burglar to think of it. The good news is the coin collection is there for the taking, and the bad news is it consists of only one coin. And the good news is that coin's worth a quarter of a million dollars, but who are you going to sell it to?

That's the bad news.

The good news is you meet a lot of people, including a fence with a sweet tooth, and a podiatrist with a great footside manner, not to mention the fence's daughter and the other burglar's sister and a gabby artist and a stolid doorman and a whole lot of cops, including the best one money can buy.

By the same author

The Burglar Who Studied Spinoza

The Burglar Who Studied Spinoza

Lawrence Block

ROBERT HALE · LONDON

Printed in Great Britain by
St Edmundsbury Press, Bury St Edmunds, Suffolk
Bound by Weatherby Woolnough

For Caryl Carnow

The Burglar Who Studied Spinoza

One

Around five-thirty I put down the book I'd been reading and started shooing customers out of the store. The book was by Robert B. Parker, and its hero was a private detective named Spenser who compensated for his lack of a first name by being terribly physical. Every couple of chapters would find him jogging around Boston or lifting weights or finding some other way to court a heart attack or a hernia. I was getting exhausted just reading about him.

My customers shooed easily enough, one pausing to buy the volume of poetry he'd been browsing, the rest melting off like a light frost on a sunny morning. I shlepped my bargain table inside ("All books 40¢ / 3 for $1"), flicked off the lights, let myself out, closed the door, locked it, drew the steel gates across the door and windows, locked them, and Barnegat Books was bedded down for the night.

My shop was closed. It was time to get down to business.

The store is on East Eleventh Street between University Place and Broadway. Two doors east is the Poodle Factory. I let myself in, heralded by the tinkling of the door chimes, and Carolyn Kaiser's head emerged from the curtain at the back. "Hi, Bern," she said. "Get comfy. I'll be right out."

I arranged myself on a pillow sofa and started leafing through a copy of a trade journal called *The Pet Dealer,* which was about what you'd expect. I thought maybe I'd see a picture of a Bouvier des Flandres, but no such luck. I was still trying when Carolyn came in carrying a very small dog the color of Old Crow and soda.

"That's not a Bouvier des Flandres," I said.

"No kidding," said Carolyn. She stood the little thing up on a table and commenced fluffing him. He looked fluffy enough to start with. "This is Prince Valiant, Bernie. He's a poodle."

"I didn't know poodles came that small."

"They keep making them smaller. He's a miniature, but he's actually smaller than the usual run of minis. I think the Japanese are getting into the field. I think they're doing something cunning with transistors."

Carolyn doesn't normally do short jokes for fear of casting the first stone. If she wore high heels she might hit five-one, but she doesn't. She has Dutch-cut dark-brown hair and Delft-blue eyes, and she's built along the lines of a fire hydrant, no mean asset in the dog-grooming trade.

"Poor Prince," she said. "The breeders keep picking out runts and cross-breeding them until they come up with something like this. And of course they breed for color, too. Prince Val's not just a mini poodle. He's an apricot mini poodle. Where the hell's his owner, anyway? What time is it?"

"Quarter to six."

"She's fifteen minutes late. Another fifteen and I'm locking up."

"What'll you do with Prince Valiant? Bring him home with you?"

"Are you kidding? The cats would eat him for breakfast. Ubi might coexist with him but Archie'd disembowel him just to keep in practice. No, if she doesn't show by six it's

4

Doggie Dannemora for the Prince. He can spend the night in a cage."

That should have been Val's cue to give a cute little yap of protest, but he just stood there like a dummy. I suggested his color was less like an apricot than a glass of bourbon and soda, and Carolyn said, "Jesus, don't remind me, I'll start drooling like one of Pavlov's finest." Then the door chimes sounded and a woman with blue-rinsed gray hair came strutting in to collect her pet.

I went back to *The Pet Dealer* while they settled Val's tab. Then his owner clipped one end of a rhinestone-studded leash to the beast's collar. They walked off together, turning east when they hit the pavement and probably bound for Stewart House, a large co-op apartment building that runs heavily to blue-rinsed gray hair, with or without an apricot poodle on the side.

"Poodles," Carolyn said. "I wouldn't have a dog because of the cats, and if I didn't have the cats I still wouldn't have a dog, but if I did it wouldn't be a poodle."

"What's wrong with poodles?"

"I don't know. Actually there's nothing wrong with standard poodles. Big black unclipped standard poodles are fine. Of course if everybody had a big black unclipped poodle I could hang up my shears and go out of business, and that might not be the worst thing in the world, anyway, come to think of it. Would you live with one of those, Bernie? A miniature poodle?"

"Well, I don't—"

"Of course you wouldn't," she said. "You wouldn't and neither would I. There are only two kinds of people who'd have a dog like that, and they're the two classes of human beings I've never been able to understand."

"How's that?"

"Gay men and straight women. Can we get out of here? I suppose I could have an apricot brandy sour. I had a lover once who used to drink them. Or I could have that bourbon

5

and soda you mentioned. But I think what I really want is a martini."

What she had was Perrier with lime.

But not without protest. Most of the protest was vented on the open air, and by the time we were at our usual table around the corner at the Bum Rap, Carolyn was agreeable if not happy about it. The waitress asked if we wanted the usual, whereupon Carolyn made a face and ordered French seltzer water, which was not her usual by any stretch of the imagination. Neither was it mine at the end of the day's work, but the day's work was not yet over. I, too, ordered Perrier, and the waitress went off scratching her head.

"See, Bern? Uncharacteristic behavior. Arouses suspicion."

"I wouldn't worry about it."

"I don't see why I can't have a real drink. The thing tonight is hours in the future. If I had a drink it would wear off in plenty of time."

"You know the rules."

"Rules."

"Without them, society would crumble. We'd have anarchy. Crime in the streets."

"Bernie—"

"Of course," I said, "I could always do a single-o tonight."

"The hell you could."

"The job wouldn't be that much harder with one than with two. I could handle it."

"Who found it in the first place?"

"You did," I said, "and you're in for fifty percent whatever happens, but you could stay home tonight and still collect it. Why run extra risks? And this way you can have your martini, or even three or four of them, and—"

"You made your point."

"I just thought—"

"I said you made your point, Bern."

6

We stopped talking while the waitress brought two glasses of Perrier to the table. On the jukebox, Loretta Lynn and Conway Twitty were singing a duet about a Mississippi woman and a Louisiana man. Perhaps it was the other way around. No matter.

Carolyn wrapped one hand around her glass and glowered at me. "I'm coming," she said.

"If you say so."

"Damn right I say so. We're partners, remember? I'm in all the way. You think because I'm a goddamn woman I should sit home keeping the goddamn home fires burning."

"I never said—"

"I don't *need* a goddamn martini." She lifted her glass. "Here's to crime, dammit." She drank it like gin.

The whole project had gotten underway at the Bum Rap, and at that very table. Carolyn and I generally get together for a drink after work, unless one or the other of us has something on, and a couple of weeks earlier we'd been raising a couple of glasses, neither of them containing Perrier water.

"It's funny how people pick dogs," Carolyn had said. "I have this one customer, her name's Wanda Colcannon, and she's got this Bouvier."

"That's funny, all right."

She looked at me. "Don't you want to hear this, Bern?"

"Sorry."

"The thing is, when she came in with the dog I figured they were a natural combination. She's a tall stern blonde out of a masochist's dream. Wears designer dresses. Cheekbones straight out of the Social Register. Yards of class, you know?"

"Uh-huh."

"And the Bouvier's a very classy dog. Very trendy these days. It's only been an AKC recognized breed for a couple of years now. They're expensive dogs, and they look pretty classy even if you don't happen to know how much they cost, and here's this leggy blonde in a leather coat with this jet-black Bouvier at her side, and they looked right for each other."

"So?"

"She picked the dog because of its name."

"What was his name?"

"Her name, not his name. The dog's a bitch."

"That's pretty trendy, too. Being a bitch."

"Oh, it never goes out of style. No, the dog's name is Astrid, as a matter of fact, but that's the name Wanda gave her. What made her pick the dog was the name of the breed."

"Why?"

"Because Wanda's maiden name is Flanders."

"Jackie Kennedy's maiden name is Bouvier," I said, "and I don't know what kind of a dog she has, and I'm not sure I care. You lost me somewhere. What does Flanders have to do with Bouvier?"

"Oh, I thought you knew. The Bouvier originated in Belgium. The full name of the breed is Bouvier des Flandres."

"Oh."

"So that's what got her interested in the breed, and she wound up buying a puppy a couple of years ago, and it turned out to be the perfect choice. She's crazy about Astrid, and the dog's incredibly devoted to her, and in addition to being a classy animal Astrid's also extremely intelligent and a great watchdog."

"I'm really happy for them," I said.

"I think you should be. I've been grooming her dog for about a year now. She'll bring her in for routine bathing and grooming every couple of months, and then she'll get the full treatment before shows. They don't show Astrid all that often but now and then they'll hit a show, and she's picked up a couple of ribbons along the way, including a blue or two."

"That's nice for her."

"For Wanda and Herb, too. Wanda loves to walk the dog. She feels safe in the streets when she's got Astrid with her. And she and her husband both feel safe with the dog guarding the house. They don't worry about burglars."

"I can understand that."

"Uh-huh. Astrid's their burglar insurance. She's due to go into heat in a couple of weeks and this time they're going to breed her. Wanda's concerned that the experience of motherhood might undercut her abilities as an attack dog, but she's going ahead with it anyway. The stud dog is a famous champion. He lives out in the country in Berks County, Pennsylvania. I think that's around Reading. They ship bitches to him from all over the country and he gets paid for it. The dog's owner gets paid, I mean."

"It's still a pretty good life for the dog."

"Isn't it? Wanda's not shipping Astrid. She and her husband are taking her out there. When you breed dogs you put the animals together two days in a row, to make sure you hit the peak ovulation period. So they'll drive out to Berks County with Astrid and stay overnight and have the second breeding the next day and drive back."

"Should make a nice trip for all three of them."

"Especially if the weather's nice."

"That's always a factor," I said. "I just know there's a reason you're telling me all this."

"Sharp of you. They'll be gone overnight, and so will Astrid, and Astrid's their burglar protection. They're rich enough to afford designer dresses and trendy purebred dogs. And for him to indulge his little hobby."

"What little hobby?"

"He collects coins."

"Oh," I said, and frowned. "You told me his name. Not Flanders, that was her maiden name, like the dog. Colcannon. But you didn't say his first name. Wait a minute. Yes, you did. His first name's Herb."

"You've got a great mind for details, Bern."

"Herb Colcannon. Herbert Colcannon. Herbert *Franklin* Colcannon. Is he *that* Herbert Colcannon?"

"How many do you figure there are?"

"He was buying proof pattern gold at a Bowers and Ruddy auction last fall and he picked up something a few months ago at a sale at Stack's. I forget what. I read something about it in *Coin World.* But the odds are he keeps the stuff in the bank."

"They've got a wall safe. What does that do to the odds?"

"Shaves them a little. How do you happen to know that?"

"She mentioned it once. How she'd wanted to wear a piece of jewelry one night and couldn't because it was locked up and she'd forgotten the combination and he was out of town. I almost told her I had a friend who could have helped her, but I decided it might be better if she didn't know about you."

"Wise decision. Maybe he doesn't keep everything in the bank. Maybe some of his coins keep her jewelry company." My mind was starting to race. Where did they live? What was the security like? How could I crack it? What was I likely to walk out with, and through whose good offices could I most expediently turn it into clean anonymous cash?

"They're in Chelsea," Carolyn went on. "Tucked away off the street in a carriage house. Not in the phone book, but I have the address. And the phone number."

"Good to have."

"Uh-huh. They have the whole house to themselves. No children. No servants living in."

"Interesting."

"I thought so. What I thought is this sounds like a job for the Dynamic Duo."

"Good thinking," I said. "I'll buy you a drink on the strength of that."

"It's about time."

Two

Illegal entry is a good deal less suspicious beneath the warm benevolent gaze of the sun. Nosy neighbors who'd dial 911 if they spotted you after dark will simply assume you've showed up at last to tend to the leaky faucet. Give me a clipboard or a toolbox and an hour between noon and four and the staunchest citizen crime-fighter on the block will hold the door for me and tell me to have a nice day. All things being equal, the best time for a residential burglary is the middle of the afternoon.

But when are all things ever equal? The cloak of darkness is comforting garb to the burglar, if not to the householder, and when one operates a legitimate business one hesitates to close it abruptly in the middle of the day for no good reason. The Colcannons' schedule, too, favored a nocturnal visit. We knew they would be away overnight, and knew too that the premises would be unencumbered by handymen or cleaning women (handy persons? cleaning persons?) once the sun was over the yardarm.

The sun had long since crossed the yardarm and disappeared somewhere in New Jersey by the time we ventured forth. From the Bum Rap we'd taken a couple of subway trains and walked a block to my building at Seventy-first and West End, where I shucked the jeans and sweater I'd worn at the store and put on flannel slacks and a tie and jacket. I filled my pockets with useful odds and ends, packed another couple of articles into my Ultrasuede attaché case, and took a moment and manicure scissors to snip the palms out of a fresh pair of rubber gloves. With rubber gloves one leaves no tattletale fingerprints behind, and with the palms out one is less likely to feel that one has abandoned one's hands in a sauna. Sweaty palms are bad enough in Lover's Lane; one tries to avoid them when burgling. Of course there's always the chance of leaving a tattletale palm print, but it wouldn't be burglary without the occasional risk, would it now?

We were almost on our way again before I remembered to change my shoes. I'd been wearing Weejun penny loafers at the store, for both nostalgia and comfort, and I switched to a pair of capable-looking Puma running shoes. I certainly had no intention of moving faster than a brisk walk, but you never know what life has in store for you, and the Pumas with their rubber soles and springy insoles let me move as soundlessly as, well, as a panther, I suppose.

Carolyn lives on Arbor Court, one of those oblique little streets in a part of the West Village that must have been laid out by someone on something stronger than Perrier. Until a couple of months ago she had been sort of living with another woman named Randy Messinger, but they'd had the last of a series of notable battles in early February and Randy had moved everything to her own place on Morton Street. It was May now, late May, and every evening the sun took a little longer to get over the yardarm, and the breach showed no signs of healing. Every now and then Carolyn would meet somebody terrific at Paula's or the Duchess, but true love had not yet bloomed, and she didn't seem to mind.

She put some coffee up, tossed a salad, warmed up a couple wedges of leftover quiche. We both ate sparingly and drank a lot of the coffee. The cats polished off their own food and rubbed against our ankles until they got the unfinished quiche, which they promptly finished. Ubi, the Russian Blue, settled in my lap and got into some serious purring. Archie, his Burmese buddy, stalked around and did some basic stretching to show off his muscles.

Around eight the phone rang. Carolyn answered it and settled into a long gossipy conversation. I got a paperback and turned its pages, but the words didn't really register. I might as well have been reading the phone book.

When Carolyn hung up I did read the phone book, long enough to look up a number, anyway. I dialed, and Abel Crowe picked up midway through the fourth ring. "Bernie," I said. "I turned up a book I think you might like. Wondered if you'd be home tonight."

"I have no plans."

"I thought I might stop by around eleven, twelve o'clock."

"Excellent. I keep late hours these days." You could hear the Mittel Europa accent over the phone. Face to face, it was barely detectable. "Will your charming friend be with you?"

"Probably."

"I'll provide accordingly. Be well, Bernard."

I hung up. Carolyn was sitting on the bed, one foot tucked beneath her, dutifully cutting the palms out of her own pair of rubber gloves. "Abel's expecting us," I told her.

"He knows I'm coming?"

"He asked specifically. I told him you'd probably show up."

"What's this probably? I love Abel."

She got up from the bed, stuffed the gloves in a back pocket. She was wearing slate-gray brushed-denim jeans and a green velour top, and now she added her navy blazer. She looked terrific, and I told her as much.

She thanked me, then turned to the cats. "Hang in there, guys," she told them. "Just write down the names if anybody calls. Tell 'em I'll get back to 'em."

*   *   *

Herbert and Wanda Colcannon lived on West Eighteenth Street between Ninth and Tenth Avenues. Until fairly recently that was a great neighborhood to visit if you were looking to get mugged, but somewhere along the line Chelsea became a desirable neighborhood. People commenced buying the old brownstones and sprucing them up, converting rooming houses into floor-through apartment buildings and apartment buildings into single-family houses. The streets were lined with newly planted ginkgo and oak and sycamore, and it was getting so that you couldn't see the muggers for the trees.

No. 442 West Eighteenth was an attractive four-story brownstone house with a mansard roof and a bay window on the parlor floor. No. 444, immediately to its left, was the same thing all over again, distinguishable only by a few minor architectural details and the pair of brass carriage lamps that flanked the entrance. But between the two houses there was an archway and a heavy iron gate, and above the gate was the number 442½. There was a bell alongside, and a blue plastic strip with the name Colcannon embossed on it beneath the bell.

I'd called the Colcannon house earlier from a pay phone on Ninth Avenue. An answering machine had invited me to leave my name and number, an invitation I'd failed to accept. Now I rang the doorbell, giving it a good long poke and waiting a full minute for a response. Beside me, Carolyn stood with her hands in her pockets and her shoulders drawn inward, shifting her weight from foot to foot.

I could imagine how she felt. This was only her third time. She'd been with me once in Forest Hill Gardens, a ritzy enclave in darkest Queens, and more recently when we hit an apartment in the East Seventies. I was an old hand at this sort of thing, I'd grown up letting myself into other people's houses, but even so the edgy anxious thrill had not worn off. I have a hunch it never will.

14

I shifted the attaché case to my left hand and dug out a ring of keys with my right. The iron gate was a formidable affair. It could be opened electrically by someone in the carriage house pushing a button, or it would yield to a key. And it was the type of old-fashioned lock that accepted a skeleton-type key, and there are only so many types, and I had a ringful of them. I'd looked the lock over some days ago and it had looked easy enough at the time, and easy it was; the third key I tried was a near miss, and the fourth one turned in the lock as if it had been placed on earth to do precisely that.

I wiped my prints off the lock and the surrounding metal, shouldered the gate open. Carolyn followed me into the covered passageway and drew the gate shut behind her. We were in a long narrow tunnel, all brick-lined and with a damp feel to it, but there was a light at the end of it and we homed in on it like moths. We came out into a garden that nestled between the brownstone in front and the Colcannons' carriage house. The light that had drawn us did a fair job of showing off the garden, with its flower beds bordering a central flagstone patio. Late daffodils and early tulips put on a good show, and I suppose when the roses bloomed the place might look fairly spectacular.

There was a semicircular bench next to what looked to be a fish pond fed by a little fountain. I wondered how they could keep fish there without their being wiped out by the local cats, and I would have enjoyed passing a few minutes on the bench, peering into the pond for signs of fish while listening to the tranquil gurgle of the fountain. But the setting was a trifle exposed for that sort of behavior.

Besides, time was a-wasting. It was twenty to ten—I'd checked my watch before unlocking the iron gate. In a sense we had all night, but the less of it we used the happier I'd be, and the sooner we'd be out of there and on our way to Abel Crowe's.

"Lit up like a Christmas tree," Carolyn said.

I looked. I hadn't paid much attention to the carriage house, intent as I was on checking out flowers and fish, and if it didn't look like a Christmas tree neither did it look like your standard empty house. It stood three stories tall, and I suppose it had once had horses on the ground floor and servants overhead before someone converted it for human occupancy throughout. Now there were lights burning on all three floors. They weren't the only source of illumination in the garden—there was also an electrified lantern mounted a few steps from the fountain—but they were probably responsible for most of the light that had reached us in the passageway.

Most people leave a light or two for the burglar, that brave little beacon that shines away at four in the morning, announcing to all the world that nobody's home. Some people improve on this with cunning little timing devices that turn the lights on and off. But Herbert and Wanda seemed to me to have gone overboard. Maybe they had overreacted to the notion of leaving the place unprotected by the noble Astrid. Maybe Herb had a ton of Con Ed stock and Wanda had overdosed on those five-year light bulbs blind people sell you over the telephone.

Maybe they were home.

I mounted the stoop and put my ear to the door. There was noise inside, radio or television, but nothing that sounded like live conversation. I rang the doorbell and listened carefully, and there was no change in the sounds within the house. I set down my attaché case and pulled on my rubber gloves while Carolyn put hers on. I said a silent prayer that the house wasn't hooked into a burglar alarm that I didn't know about, addressing the prayer to Saint Dismas. He's the patron saint of thieves, and he must get to hear a lot of prayers these days.

Let there not be a burglar alarm, I urged the good Dismas. Let the dog really be in Pennsylvania. Let what lies within be a burglar's fondest dream, and in return I'll—I'll what?

I took out my ring of picks and probes and went to work. The locks were pretty good. There were three of them on that door, two Segals and a Rabson. I left the Rabson for last because I knew it would be the toughest, then surprised myself by knocking it off in no more than a minute. I heard Carolyn's intake of breath when the bolt turned. She knows a little about locks now, and has been known to open her own without a key, and she's driven herself half mad practicing with a Rabson I gave her, and she sounded impressed.

I turned the knob, opened the door a crack, stood aside for Carolyn. She shook her head and motioned for me to go first. Age before beauty? Pearls before swine? Death before dishonor? I opened the door and committed illegal entry.

Lord, what a feeling!

I'm grateful there isn't something even more despicable than burglary that gives me that feeling, because if there were I probably wouldn't be able to resist it. Oh, I'm a pro, all right, and I do it for the money, but let's not kid ourselves. I draw such an intense charge out of it it's a wonder lamps don't dim all over the city every time I let myself into somebody else's abode.

God knows I'm not proud of it. I'd think far more highly of myself if I eked out a living at Barnegat Books. I never quite cover expenses at the store, but maybe I could if I took the trouble to learn to be a better businessman. The shop supported old Mr. Litzauer for years before he sold it to me and retired to St. Petersburg. It ought to be able to support me. I don't live all that high. I don't shoot crap or snort coke or zoom around with the Beautiful People. Nor do I consort with known criminals, as the parole board so charmingly phrases it. I don't like criminals. I don't like being one myself.

But I love to steal. Go figure.

The radio program was one of those talk-show things with listeners calling in to share their views on fluoridation and child labor and other burning issues. I stood there and resented its blaring away at me. The lights were a nice touch —we wouldn't have to turn on lights ourselves, which might draw attention, nor would we have to curse the darkness. But I stood there in the entrance foyer and resolved to turn off the damned radio. It was a distraction. You have to think straight to burgle efficiently, and who could do so with all that noise?

"Jesus, Bern."

"What?"

"She always dresses so nice. Who figured she'd be such a slob around the house?"

I followed her into the living room to see what she was talking about. It looked as though an out-of-season tropical storm had wandered far off course, only to sneak down through the chimney and kick the crap out of everything. The pillows were off the couch. Desk drawers had been pulled out and upended, their contents strewn all over the Aubusson carpet. Pictures had been taken down from the walls, books tossed from their shelves.

"Burglars," I said.

Carolyn stared.

"They beat us to the punch."

"Are they still around, Bern? We better get out of here."

I went back to the front door and checked it. I'd relocked the locks when we were inside, fastening an additional chain lock for good measure. The three locks had been locked when I found them, the chain bolt unengaged.

Strange.

If burglars had come through that door, and if they'd locked themselves in as I had done, wouldn't they put the chain bolt on as well? And if they'd already left, would they bother locking up from outside? I generally do that sort of thing as a matter of course, but then I'm not apt to leave a room looking as though it had been visited by the Gadarene swine, either. Whoever tossed that room was the type who kicked doors in, not the type who took extra time to lock up afterward.

Unless—

Lots of possibilities. I eased past Carolyn and began tracking the radio to its source. I passed through the dining room, where a mahogany breakfront and buffet had been rifled in fashion similar to the living-room desk, and entered a kitchen that had received a dose of the same treatment. A Panasonic stood on the butcher-block counter beside the refrigerator, blaring its transistorized heart out. I turned to Carolyn, raised a finger to my lips for silence, and switched off the radio in the middle of a rant about the latest increase in the price of oil.

I closed my eyes and listened very carefully to the ensuing silence. You could have heard a pin drop, and I was certain no one had dropped one.

"They're gone," I said.

"How can you be sure?"

"If they were here we'd hear them. They're not the silent type, whoever they are."

"We better get out."

"Not yet."

"Are you crazy, Bern? If they're gone, that just means the cops are on their way, and even if they're not, what are we gonna find to steal? Whoever did this already took everything."

"Not necessarily."

"Well, they took the sterling. What are we gonna do, swipe the stainless?" She followed me out of the kitchen and up a flight of stairs. "What do you expect to find, Bern?"

"A coin collection. Maybe some jewelry."

"Where?"

"Good question. What room is the wall safe in?"

"I don't know."

"Then we'll have to look for it, won't we?"

We didn't have to look very hard because our predecessors

in crime had taken all the pictures off the walls. We checked the library and guest bedroom on the second floor, then climbed another flight of stairs and found the wall safe in the master bedroom. The dreamy pastoral landscape which had screened it from view was on the floor now, along with the contents of both dressers and some broken glass from the overhead skylight. That, no doubt, was how they'd entered. And how they'd exited as well, I felt certain, lugging their loot across the rooftops and into the night. These clowns hadn't locked up downstairs because they'd never opened the locks in the first place. They couldn't have dealt with that Rabson in a year and a day.

Nor had they been able to deal with the wall safe. I'm not sure how hard they tried. There were marks around the combination dial to show that someone had worked on it with a punch, hoping to knock the lock out and get into the safe that way. I didn't see any evidence that they'd had an acetylene torch along, nor would one very likely have worked anyway. The safe was a sound one and the lock was a beauty.

I commenced fiddling with the dial. Carolyn stood beside me, watching with more than idle curiosity, but before long we started to fidget and we were getting on each other's nerves. Before I could suggest it she said something about having a look around. I promised to call her when I got the thing open.

It took a little doing. I stripped off my rubber gloves—that Jimmy Valentine number of sanding one's fingertips for increased sensitivity is nonsense, but there's no point in making things more difficult than they have to be. I did a little of this and a little of that, using the combination of knowledge and intuition that you have to have if you're going to be good with locks, and I got the last number first, as one always does with combination locks, and one at a time I got the other three numbers, and then I put my gloves on again and wiped the surfaces I'd touched and took a deep breath and whistled for Carolyn.

She came in carrying a framed print. "It's a Chagall litho-graph," she said. "Pencil-signed and numbered. I guess it's worth a few hundred, anyway. Is it worth stealing?"

"If you want to take it out of the frame."

She held it up. "I think it'll fit in the attaché case. Are you getting anywhere with that mother?"

"I'm just going to try a couple numbers at random," I said. I dialed the four numbers in their proper sequence, felt a little click in my own head if not in the locking mechanism as the tumblers lined up, then swung the handle around to the left and opened the safe.

We left the house as we'd entered it. I suppose we could have gone over the rooftops ourselves, but why? I paused in the kitchen to turn the radio on again. A commercial was offering a three-LP set of the hundred greatest rumba and samba hits. There was a toll-free number to call, but I ne-glected to jot it down. I unhooked the chain bolt and un-locked three locks, and out we went, and I let Carolyn hold the attaché case while I used my ring of picks and probes to manipulate all three locks shut again. In school they taught me that neatness counts, and the lessons you learn early in life stay with you.

The fountain was still gurgling and the little garden was still being charming. I stripped off my rubber gloves, tucked them into a back pocket. Carolyn did the same with hers. I retrieved the attaché case and we made our way through the dark tunnel to the heavy iron gate. You didn't need a key to let yourself out—there was a knob to turn, unreachable from the street side. I turned it and let us out, and the gate swung shut and locked after us.

On the other side of the street, a slender young man with a wad of paper towel in his hand was bending over to clean up after his Airedale. He took no notice of us and we headed off in the opposite direction.

At the corner of Ninth Avenue Carolyn said, "Somebody else must have known about their trip. That they were taking the dog and all. Unless someone was just going over the roofs and got lucky."

"Not very likely."

"No. Wanda must have told someone else. Nobody heard it from me, Bernie."

"People talk," I said, "and a good burglar learns how to listen. If we'd gotten there first we'd have scored a lot bigger, but this way we can travel light. And we're free and clear, look at it that way. Those clowns went through that poor house like Cromwell's men at Drogheda, and it shouldn't take the cops too long to catch up with them. And we didn't leave a trace, so they'll hang the whole thing on them."

"I thought of that. What did you think of the Chagall?"

"I hardly looked at it."

"I was wondering how it would look in my apartment."

"Where?"

"I was thinking maybe over the wicker chair."

"Where you've got the Air India poster now?"

"Yeah. I was thinking maybe it's time I outgrew my travel poster phase. I might want to have the litho rematted, but that's no big deal."

"We'll see how it looks."

"Yeah." Three cabs sailed by, all with their off-duty signs lit. "I just took it because I wanted to take something, you know? I didn't want to leave empty-handed."

"I know."

"I had figured you'd be cracking the safe while I went through the drawers, but some bastards already went through the drawers and there was nothing for me to do. I felt sort of out of it."

"I can imagine."

"So I stole the Chagall."

"It'll probably look terrific over the chair, Carolyn."

"Well, we'll see."

Three

Abel Crowe lived in one of those towering prewar apartment buildings on Riverside Drive. Our taxi let us out in front and we walked around the corner to the entrance on Eighty-ninth Street. The doorman was planted in the entranceway, holding his post like Horatius at the bridge. His face was a glossy black, his uniform a rich cranberry shade. It sported more gold braid than your average rear admiral and he wore it with at least as much pride of place.

He gave Carolyn a quick look-see, then checked me out from haircut to Pumas. He did not appear impressed. He was no more moved by my name, and while Abel Crowe's name didn't quite strike him with awe, either, at least it took the edge off his hostility. He rang upstairs on the intercom, spoke briefly into the mouthpiece, then informed us we were expected.

"Apartment 11-D," he said, and waved us on to the elevator.

A lot of those buildings have converted to self-service elevators as a means of cutting overhead in the name of modernization, but Abel's building had gone co-op a few years ago and the tenants were big on keeping up the old standards. The elevator attendant wore a uniform like the doorman's but didn't fill it nearly so well. He was a runty wheyfaced youth with a face that had never seen the sun, and about him there hung an aroma that gave the lie to the advertiser's assurance that vodka leaves you breathless. He did his job, though, wafting us ten flights above sea level and waiting to see that we went to the designated apartment, and that the tenant was happy to see us.

There was no question about that last point.

"My dear Bernard!" Abel cried out, gripping me urgently by the shoulders. "And the beloved Carolyn!" He let go of me and embraced my partner in crime. "I'm so glad you could come," he said, ushering us inside. "It is half past eleven. I was beginning to worry."

"I said between eleven and twelve, Abel."

"I know, Bernard, I know, and all the same I began at half past ten to check my watch, and I seemed to be doing so every three minutes. But come in, come in, let us make ourselves comfortable. I have a house full of wonderful things to eat. And of course you'll want something to drink."

"Of course we will," Carolyn agreed.

He took a moment to lock up, sliding the massive bolt of the Fox lock into its mount on the jamb. Fox makes a couple of police locks. The kind I have features a five-foot steel bar fixed at a forty-five-degree angle between a plate set into the floor and a catch on the door. Abel's was a simpler mechanism but almost as good insurance against somebody's knocking the door down with anything lighter than a medieval battering ram. It featured a bolt two feet long and a good inch wide, made of tempered steel and mounted securely on the door and sliding sideways to engage an equally solid catch on the doorjamb. I'd learned on a previous visit that an identical lock secured the apartment's other door, the one leading to the service area and freight elevator.

I don't suppose most of the tenants bothered with such heavy-duty locks, not in a building so well protected by the staff. But Abel had his reasons.

His occupation, for one. Abel was a fence, and probably the best in the New York area when it came to top-quality collections of rare stamps and coins. He would take other things as well—jewelry, objets d'art—but stamps and coins were the sort of stolen goods he was happiest to receive.

Fences are natural targets for thieves. You'd think they'd be off-limits, that criminals would forbear to bite the hands that feed them, but it doesn't work that way. A fence generally has something on hand worth stealing—either goods he's lately purchased or the cold cash with which he conducts all his business. Perhaps as important, he can't complain to the police. As a result, most of the fences I know live in fully serviced buildings, double-lock their doors, and tend to have a gun or two within easy reach.

On the other hand, Abel might have been almost as security-conscious however he earned his living. He had spent the Second World War in Dachau, and not as a guard. I can understand how the experience might leave one with a slight streak of healthy paranoia.

Abel's living room, richly paneled in dark woods and lined with bookshelves, looks westward over Riverside Park and the Hudson River to New Jersey. Almost a year earlier, on the Fourth of July, the three of us had watched the Macy's fireworks display from Abel's windows, listening to a radio broadcast of classical music with which the fireworks were presumably coordinated and putting away vast quantities of pastry.

We were seated in the same fashion now, Carolyn and I with glasses of Scotch, Abel with a mug of espresso topped with fresh whipped cream. WNCN was playing a Haydn string quartet for us, and outside there was nothing more spectacular to watch than the cars on the West Side Highway and the joggers circumvolving the park. No doubt some of the latter had shoes just like mine.

When Haydn gave way to Vivaldi, Abel set his empty mug aside and leaned back in his chair with his pink hands folded over his ample abdomen. Only his midsection was fat; his hands and arms were lean, and there was not much spare flesh on his face. But he had a Santa Claus belly and upper thighs that bulged in his blue gabardine trousers, attributes quite consistent with his boundless enthusiasm for rich desserts.

According to him, he had never been fat until after the war. "When I was in the camps," he had told me once, "I thought constantly of meat and potatoes. I dreamed of fat sausages and great barons of beef. Crown roasts of pork. Kids roasted whole on a spit. Meanwhile I grew gaunt and my skin shrank on my bones like leather left to dry in the sun. When the American forces liberated the camps they weighed us. God knows why. Most fat men claim to be large-boned. Doubtless some of them are. I have small bones, Bernard. I tipped the scales, as they say, at ninety-two pounds.

"I left Dachau clinging to one certainty. I was going to eat and grow fat. And then I discovered, to my considerable astonishment, that I had no interest in the meat and potatoes I had grown up on. That SS rifle butts had relieved me of my own teeth was only a partial explanation, for I had for meat itself a positive aversion—I could not eat a sausage without feeling I was biting into a plump Teutonic finger. And yet I had an appetite, a bottomless one, but it was a most selective and specific appetite. I wanted sugar. I craved sweetness. Is there anything half so satisfying as knowing precisely what one wishes and being able to obtain it? If I could afford it, Bernard, I would engage a live-in pastry cook and keep him occupied around the clock."

He'd had a piece of Linzer torte with his coffee and had offered us a choice of half a dozen decadently rich pastries, all of which we'd passed for the time being while we tended to our drinks.

"Ah, Bernard," he said now. "And the lovely Carolyn. It is so very good to see you both. But the night is growing old, isn't it? You have brought me something, Bernard?"

My attaché case was close at hand. I opened it and drew out a compact volume of Spinoza's *Ethics,* an English edition printed in London in 1707 and bound in blue calf. I passed it to Abel and he turned it over and over in his hands, stroking the smooth old leather with his long and slender fingers, studying the title page at some length, flipping through the pages.

He said, "Regard this, if you will. 'It is the part of the wise man to feed himself with moderate pleasant food and drink, and to take pleasure with perfumes, with the beauty of living plants, dress, music, sport and theaters, and other places of this sort which man may use without any injury to his fellows.' If Baruch Spinoza were in this room I'd cut him a generous piece of Linzer torte, and I don't doubt he'd relish it." He returned to the title page. "This is quite nice," he allowed. "1707. I have an early edition in Latin, printed in Amsterdam. The first edition was when, 1675?"

"1677."

"My own copy is dated 1683, I believe. The only copy I own in English is the Everyman's Library edition with the Boyle translation." He moistened a finger, turned some more pages. "Quite nice. A little water damage, a few pages foxed, but quite nice for all that." He read to himself for a moment, then closed the book with a snap. "I might find a spot for this on my shelves," he said carelessly. "Your price, Bernard?"

"It's a gift."

"For me?"

"If you can find a spot for it. On your shelves."

He colored. "But I expected no such thing! And here am I, mean-spirited enough to point out water damage and the odd foxed page as if to lay the groundwork for some hard bargaining. Your generosity shames me, Bernard. It's a splendid little volume, the binding's really quite gorgeous, and I'm thrilled to have it. You're quite certain you don't want any money for it?"

I shook my head. "It came into the store with a load of fine bindings, decorator specials with nothing substantial between the covers. You wouldn't believe what people have seen fit to wrap in leather down through the years. And I can sell anything with a decent binding. Interior decorators buy them by the yard. I was sorting this lot and I spotted the Spinoza and thought of you."

"You are kind and thoughtful," he said, "and I thank you." He drew a breath, let it out, turned to place the book on the table beside his empty mug. "But Spinoza alone did not bring you out at this hour. You have brought me something else, have you not?"

"Three things, actually."

"And they will not be gifts."

"Not quite."

I took a small velvet bag from the attaché case, handed it to him. He weighed it in his hand, then spilled its contents into his palm. A pair of teardrop earrings, emeralds, quite simple and elegant. Abel drew a jeweler's loupe from his breast pocket and fixed it in his eye. While he was squinting through it at the stones, Carolyn crossed to the sideboard where the liquor and pastries were laid out. She freshened her drink. She was back in her chair and her glass was a third empty by the time Abel was through examining the emerald earrings.

"Good color," he said. "Slight flaws. Not garbage, Bernard, but nothing extraordinary, either. Did you have a figure in mind?"

"I never have a figure in mind."

"You should keep these. Carolyn should wear them. Model them for us, *liebchen.*"

"I don't have pierced ears."

"You should. Every woman should have pierced lobes, and emerald teardrops to wear in them. Bernard, I wouldn't care to pay more than a thousand for these. I think that's high. I'm basing that figure on a retail estimate of five thousand, and the true price might be closer to four. I will pay a thousand, Bernard. No more than that."

"Then a thousand is the price."

"Done," he said, and returned the earrings to their velvet bag and placed the bag on top of Spinoza's *Ethics*. "You have something else?"

I nodded and took a second velvet bag from the attaché case. It was blue—the one with the earrings had been the color of the doorman's uniform—and it was larger, and equipped with a drawstring. Abel undrew the string and took out a woman's wristwatch with a rectangular case, a round dial, and a gold mesh band. I don't know that he needed the loupe, but he fixed it in his eye all the same and took a close look.

"Piaget," he said. "What time do you have, Bernard?"

"Twelve oh seven."

"Mr. Piaget agrees with you to the minute." I wasn't surprised; I'd wound and set the watch when I took it from the safe. "You'll excuse me for a moment? I just want to look at a recent catalog. And won't you help yourselves to some of those pastries? I have eclairs, I have Sacher torte, I have Schwarzwälder kuchen. Have something sweet, both of you. I'll be with you in a moment."

I broke down and took an eclair. Carolyn selected a wedge of seven-layer cake with enough chocolate between the layers to make an entire high school class break out. I filled two mugs with coffee and two small snifters with tawny Armagnac that was older than we were. Abel came back, visibly pleased to see us eating, and announced that the retail price of the watch was $4,950. That was a little higher than I'd thought.

"I can pay fifteen hundred," he said. "Because I can turn it over so quickly and easily. Satisfactory?"

"Satisfactory."

"That's twenty-five hundred so far. You said three items, Bernard? The first two are nice merchandise, but I hope they don't represent too great an investment of time and effort on your part. Are you sure you wouldn't prefer to keep them? Ears can be pierced readily enough, and painlessly, I'm told. And wouldn't the watch grace your wrist, Carolyn?"

"I'd have to keep taking it off every time I washed a dog."

"I hadn't thought of that." He grinned widely. "What I should do," he said, "is put aside both of these articles and make you a present of them when the two of you get married. I'd have to find something suitable for you as well, Bernard, though wedding presents are really for the bride, don't you think? What about it, Carolyn? Shall I put these away?"

"You'd have a long wait, Abel. We're just good friends."

"And business associates, eh?"

"That too."

He chuckled heartily and sat back and folded his hands once again on his belly, an expectant look on his face. I let him wait. Then he said, "You said you had three items."

"Two earrings and a watch."

"Ah, my mistake. I thought the earrings counted as a single unit. Then the total sum is twenty-five hundred dollars."

"Well, there is something else you might want to look at," I said carelessly, and from the attaché case I produced a brown kraft envelope two inches square. Abel shot me a look, then took the envelope from me. Inside it was a hinged Plexiglas box just small enough to fit into the envelope, and inside that was a wad of tissue paper. Abel opened the tissue paper very deliberately, his fingers moving with the precision of one accustomed to handling rare coins. When a nick or a scratch can reduce a coin's value substantially, when a finger mark can begin the hateful process of corrosion, one learns to grasp coins by their edges and to hold them gently but securely.

The object Abel Crowe held gently but securely between the thumb and index finger of his left hand was a metallic disc just under seven-eighths of an inch in diameter—or just over two centimeters, if you're into metrics. It was, in short, the size and shape of a nickel, the sort of nickel that's the price of the good cigar this country is purported to need. It was the color of a nickel, too, although its frosted features and mirrorlike field were a ways removed from anything you'd be likely to have in your pocket.

By and large, though, it looked like a nickel. And well it might, for that was precisely what it was.

All it lacked was Thomas Jefferson's head on the one side and his house on the other. The side Abel looked at first showed a large V within a wreath open at the top, the word *Cents* inscribed directly beneath the V. Circling the wreath were the issuing nation's name and motto—*United States of America* above, *E Pluribus Unum* below.

Abel flicked me a glance from beneath upraised eyebrows, then deftly turned the coin in his fingers. Its obverse depicted a woman's head facing left, her coronet inscribed *Liberty*. Thirteen stars circled Miss Liberty, and beneath her head was the date.

"Gross Gott!" said Abel Crowe. And then he closed his eyes and said another long sentence that I didn't understand, possibly in German, possibly in some other language.

Carolyn looked at me, her expression quizzical. "Is that good or bad?" she wanted to know.

I told her I wasn't sure.

Four

He didn't say anything else until he'd looked long and hard at both sides of the coin through his jeweler's loupe. Then he wrapped the coin in tissue paper, returned it to the Plexiglas box and tucked the box into the kraft envelope, which he placed on the table beside him. With an effort he heaved himself out of his chair to fetch another slab of nutritionist's nightmare and a fresh cup of coffee *mit schlag*. He sat down, ate for a while, set his plate down half finished, sipped the coffee through the thick whipped cream, and glared at me.

"Well?" he demanded. "Is it genuine?"

"I just steal them," I said. "I don't authenticate them. I suppose I could have dropped in on Walter Breen or Don Taxay for a professional opinion, but I figured it was late."

His glance moved to Carolyn. "You know about this coin?"

"He never tells me anything."

"A Liberty Head Nickel," he said. "Nickel five-cent pieces were first issued in this country in 1866. The original design showed a shield. In 1883 the government switched to this design, although the initial run of coins lacked the word *cents* on the reverse. There was thus some confusion as to the coin's denomination, and it was cleverly compounded by those who filed the edge of the coin to simulate the milling on a gold coin, then plated it lightly with gold and passed it as a five-dollar gold piece."

He paused and had himself a sip of coffee, used a napkin to blot a thin line of whipped cream from his upper lip. "The coin was issued without interruption through 1912," he continued. "In 1913 it was replaced by the Buffalo Nickel. The Mint had problems with that issue, too, in the first year. Originally the mound on which the bison stands was in excessive relief and the coins would not stack properly. This was corrected, but the dates of these coins tended to wear off prematurely. It was a poor design.

"But I am telling you more than you would care to know. The last Liberty Head Nickels, or V-Nickels, as they are sometimes called, were struck in Philadelphia and Denver and San Francisco in 1912." He paused again, breathed in, breathed out. "The specimen you were so kind as to bring me tonight," he said, "is dated 1913."

"That must make it special," Carolyn said.

"You might say that. Five specimens of the 1913 V-Nickel are known to exist. They are clearly a product of the U.S. Mint, although the Mint has always denied having produced them.

"It is fairly clear what must have happened. Dies for a 1913 V-Nickel must have been prepared before the decision to switch to the buffalo design was finalized. Possibly a few pieces were struck as die trials; alternately, an enterprising employee may have produced these trial pieces on his own initiative. In any event, five specimens left the Mint by the back door."

He sighed, removed one of his slippers, massaged his arch. "I carry too much weight," he said. "It is alleged to endanger the heart. My heart makes no objection but my feet protest incessantly.

"But no matter. Let us return to the year 1913. At the time, a gentleman named Samuel Brown worked at the Mint in Philadelphia. He left shortly thereafter and next emerged in North Tonawanda, a suburb of Buffalo, where he placed advertisements seeking to buy 1913 Liberty Head Nickels—which of course no one had heard of at the time. He subsequently announced that he had managed to purchase five such nickels, and those are the only five which were ever to see the light of day. Perhaps you can guess how he happened to get them."

"He walked out of the Mint with them," I said, "and the ads were his way of explaining his ownership of the coins."

Abel nodded. "And his way of publicizing them in the bargain. You are familiar with the name of E. H. R. Green? Colonel Edward Green? His mother was Hetty Green, the notorious witch of Wall Street, and when her son came into his money he was able to indulge his eccentricities, one of which was numismatics. He did not wish merely one specimen of a rarity; he wanted as many as he could lay hands on. Accordingly, he bought all five of Samuel Brown's 1913 V-Nickels.

"They remained in his possession until his death, and I trust he enjoyed owning them. When he died his holdings were dispersed, and a dealer named Johnson wound up with all five of the nickels. I believe he lived in the Midwest, St. Louis or perhaps Kansas City."

"It doesn't matter," I said.

"Probably not," he agreed. "In any event, Mr. Johnson sold them off one at a time to individual collectors. While he was doing this, a dealer in Fort Worth by the name of B. Max Mehl was busy making the 1913 V-Nickel the most famous rare coin of the century simply by offering to buy it. He placed advertisements everywhere offering fifty dollars for the coin, with the implication that one might come across it in one's pocket change. He did so in order to attract custom-

34

ers for a rare coin catalogue he was peddling, and I don't doubt he sold a great many catalogues, but in the course of it he assured the future of the 1913 nickel. No American coin ever received so much publicity. Americans who knew nothing else about coins knew a 1913 V-Nickel was valuable. Virtually everyone knew this."

I did. I remembered the ads he was talking about. They were still running when I was a boy, and I was one of the guppies who sent for the book. None of us found 1913 V-Nickels in our pockets, since they weren't there to be found, but many of us began collecting coins and grew up to swell the ranks of the numismatic fraternity. Others of us grew up to be thieves, seeking our fortunes in other men's pocket change, as it were.

"There's no logical explanation for the coin's value," Abel went on. "At best it's a trial piece, at worst an unauthorized fantasy item. As such it should be worth a few thousand dollars at most. The Mint struck pattern nickels in 1881 and 1882 in a variety of metals and with a variety of designs. Some are as rare or rarer than the 1913 nickel, yet you can buy them for a few hundred dollars. In 1882 a pattern coin was struck identical in design to the V-Nickel, and in the same metal, but with that year's date. It's quite rare, and if anything it ought to be more desirable than the 1913 coin, if only because its existence is legitimate. Yet a couple of thousand dollars will buy it, assuming you can locate an example for sale."

Carolyn's face was showing a lot of excitement about now, and I could understand why. If another coin was worth a couple of thousand, and that made it strictly minor-league compared to what we'd come up with, then we were in good shape. But she still didn't know just how good that shape was. She was waiting for him to tell her.

He made her wait. He reached for his plate, finished his pastry, switched plate for cup, drank coffee. Carolyn got herself more Armagnac, drank some of it, watched him sip his coffee, drank the rest of the Armagnac, made her hands into fists, planted them on her hips, and said, "Aw, come on, Abel. What's it worth?"

"I don't know."

"Huh?"

"No one knows. Maybe you should put it in a parking meter. Bernard, why did you bring me this?"

"Well, it seemed like a good idea at the time, Abel. If you want I'll take it home with me."

"And do what with it?"

"I don't have a car so I won't put it in a parking meter. Maybe I'll punch a hole in it and Carolyn can wear it around her neck."

"I almost wish you would do that."

"Or maybe somebody else'll buy it."

"Who? To whom would you offer it? No one will deal more equitably with you than I, Bernard."

"That's why I brought it to you in the first place, Abel."

"Yes, yes, of course." He sighed, fished out a handkerchief, wiped his high forehead. "The *verdammte* coin has agitated me. What is it worth? Who *knows* what the thing is worth? Five specimens exist. As I recall, four are in museum collections, only one in private hands. I remember seeing a 1913 V-Nickel just once in my life. It was perhaps fifteen years ago. A gentleman named J. V. McDermott owned it and he liked to exhibit his treasure. He put it on display at coin shows whenever asked, and the rest of the time he was apt to carry it around in his pocket and show it to people. Few collectors get the pleasure out of their possession that Mr. McDermott derived from his nickel.

"When the coin passed into another pair of hands it brought fifty thousand dollars, as I recall. There have been sales since. In 1976, I believe it was, a 1913 nickel changed hands for a hundred and thirty thousand. I don't remember if it was the McDermott coin or not. It might have been.

More recently there was a private sale reported with an announced figure of two hundred thousand."

Carolyn put her glass to her lips, tipped it up. She didn't seem to notice that there was nothing in it. Her eyes were on Abel, and they were as wide as I had ever seen them.

He sighed. "What do you want for this coin, Bernard?"

"Wealth beyond the dreams of avarice."

"A felicitious phrase. Your own?"

"Samuel Johnson said it first."

"I thought it had a classic ring to it. Spinoza called avarice 'nothing but a species of madness, although not enumerated among diseases.' Are you mad enough yourself to have a price in mind?"

"No."

"It's so difficult to put a value on the damned thing. When they sold the John Work Garrett collection, a Brasher doubloon brought seven hundred twenty-five thousand. What might this coin bring at auction? Half a million? It's possible. It's not sane, not by any means, but it's possible nevertheless."

Carolyn, glassy-eyed, went for more Armagnac. "But you can't consign this piece for auction sale," he continued, "and neither can I. Where did it come from?"

I hesitated, but only for a moment. "A man named Colcannon owned it," I said, "until a couple of hours ago."

"H. F. Colcannon? I know of him, of course, but I didn't know he bought the 1913 nickel. When did he acquire it?"

"No idea."

"What else did you get from him?"

"Two earrings and a watch. There was nothing else in his safe except legal papers and stock certificates, and I left them as I found them."

"There were no other coins?"

"None."

"But—" He frowned. "The V-Nickel," he said. "Didn't he

37

have it in a frame or a custom lucite holder or something of the sort?"

"It was just as I gave it to you. Tissue paper and a hinged box in a two-by-two coinvelope."

"Remarkable."

"I thought so."

"Simply remarkable. He must have just purchased it. You found it in a safe in his home? He must keep his holdings in a bank vault. Is this the McDermott coin, do you know? Or did one of the museums sell it? Museums don't hold on to things forever, you know. They don't just buy. They sell things off now and then, although they prefer to call it de-accessioning, which is a particularly choice example of new-speak, don't you think? Where did Herbert Colcannon get this coin?"

"Abel, I didn't even know he had it until I found it in his safe."

"Yes, of course." He reached for the coin, opened the envelope, unwrapped a half million dollars' worth of nickel. With the loupe in one eye and the other squeezed shut in a squint, he said, "I don't think it's counterfeit. Counterfeits exist, you know. One takes a nickel from 1903, say, or 1910 or '11 or '12, grinds off the inappropriate digit and solders on a replacement removed from another coin. But there would be visible evidence of such tampering on a coin in proof condition, and I see no such evidence here. Besides, it would cost you several hundred dollars for a proof common-date V-Nickel to practice on. I'm almost certain it's genuine. An X-ray would help, or the counsel of an expert numisma-tist."

He sighed gently. "At a more favorable hour I could estab-lish the coin's bona fides without leaving this building. But at this time of night let us merely assume the coin is genuine. To whom could I sell it? And for what price? It would have to go to a collector who would be willing to own it anony-mously, one who could accept the fact that open resale would be forever impossible. Art collectors of this stripe abound; the pleasure they take in their paintings seems to be heightened by their illegitimate provenance. But coin collectors respond less to the aesthetic beauty of an object and more to the prestige and profit that accompany it. Who would buy this piece? Oh, there are collectors who'd be glad to have it, but which of them might I approach and what might I ask?"

I got some more coffee. I started to pour a little Armagnac into it to give it a bit more authority, then told myself the Armagnac was entirely too good to be so dealt with. And then I reminded myself that I had just lifted a half-million-dollar coin, so why was I holding back on some thirty-bucks-a-bottle French brandy? I laced my coffee with it and took a sip, and it warmed me clear down to my toes.

"You have three choices," Abel said.

"Oh?"

"One: You can take the coin home with you and enjoy the secret ownership of an object more valuable than you are ever likely to own again. This coin is worth at least a quarter of a million, perhaps twice that, possibly even more. And I have been holding it in my hand. Extraordinary, is it not? For a few hours' work, you can have the pleasure of holding it in your own hands whenever you want."

"What are my other choices?"

"Two: You can sell it to me tonight. I'll give you cash, unrecorded fifties and hundreds. You'll leave here with the money in your pocket."

"How much, Abel?"

"Fifteen thousand dollars."

"For a coin worth half a million."

He let that pass. "Three: You can leave the coin with me. I will sell it for what I can and I will give you half of whatever I receive. I'll take my time, but I'll certainly endeavor to move the coin as quickly as possible. Perhaps I'll find a customer. Perhaps the *verdammte* thing's insured by a carrier with a policy of repurchasing stolen goods. It's a delicate

39

business, dealing with those companies. You can't always trust them. If it was a recent acquisition, Colcannon may not even have insured it yet. Perhaps he never insures his coins, perhaps he regards his safe-deposit box as insurance enough, and intended placing this coin there after he'd had an appropriate case made for it."

He spread his hands, sighed heavily. "Perhaps, perhaps, perhaps. Dozens of perhapses. I'm an old man, Bernard. Take the coin with you tonight and save me a headache. What do I need with the aggravation? I have enough money."

"What will you try to sell it for?"

"I already told you I don't know. You want a rough estimate? I shall pluck a figure out of the air, then, and say a hundred thousand dollars. A nice round number. The final price might be a great deal more or a great deal less, depending on circumstances, but you ask me to come up with a figure and that is the figure that comes to mind."

"A hundred thousand."

"Perhaps."

"And our half would be fifty thousand."

"And to think you made the calculation without pencil and paper, Bernard."

"And if we take the cash tonight?"

"What sum did I offer? Fifteen thousand. Plus the twenty-five hundred I owe you for the earrings and the watch. That would total seventeen-five." No pencil and paper for him, either. We were a couple of mathematical wizards. "I'll tell you what. Let's deal in round numbers tonight. Twenty thousand dollars for everything."

"Or twenty-five hundred now plus half of what you get for the coin."

"If I get anything for it. If it proves to be genuine, and if I find someone who wants it."

"You wouldn't care to make it three thousand for the watch and earrings plus a split on the coin?"

He thought a moment. "No," he said, "I wouldn't want to do that, Bernard."

I looked at Carolyn. We could walk away with ten thou apiece for the night's work or settle for a little over a tenth of that plus a shot at wealth beyond the etc. I asked her what she thought.

"Up to you, Bern."

"I just wondered what—"

"Uh-uh. Up to you."

Take the money and run, a voice whispered in my head. Take the cash and let the credit go. A bird in the hand is worth two in the bush. The voice that whispers in my head isn't terribly original, but it does tend to cut to the heart of the matter.

But did I want to be known as the man who got a hot ten grand for the Colcannon V-Nickel? And how happy would I be with my ten thousand dollars when I thought of Abel Crowe getting a six-figure price for it?

I could have topped his Spinoza quote. *"Pride, Envy and Avarice are the three sparks that have set the hearts of all on fire."* From the Sixth Canto of Dante's *Inferno.*

My heart burned from all three, not to mention the eclair and the Armagnac. "We'll take the twenty-five hundred," I told him.

"If you want more time to think about it—"

"The last thing I want is more time to think about it."

He smiled. He looked like a benevolent grandfather again, honest as any man living. "I'll be just a moment," he said, getting to his feet. "There's more food, more coffee, plenty to drink. Help yourselves."

While he was in the other room Carolyn and I had one short drink apiece to toast the night's work. Then Abel returned and counted out a stack of twenty-five bills. He said he hoped we didn't mind hundreds. Not at all, I assured him; I wished I had a million of them. He chuckled politely.

"Take care of our nickel," I urged. "There's thieves everywhere."

"They could never get in here."

"Gordius thought nobody could untie that knot, remember? And the Trojans were suckers for a horse."

"And pride goeth before a fall, eh?" He laid a reassuring hand on my shoulder. "The doormen are very security-conscious here. The elevator is always attended. And you have seen the police locks on my doors."

"What about the fire escape?"

"It is on the front of the building, where anyone using it could be seen from the street. The window that opens onto it is secured by steel gates. I can assure you no one could get in that way. I only hope I could get out if there were ever a fire." He smiled. "In any event, Bernard, I shall conceal the nickel where no one will think to look for it. And no one will know I have it in the first place."

Five

I'm not entirely sure why I wound up spending what was left of the night at Carolyn's. All that sugar and caffeine and alcohol, plus enough tension and excitement for your average month, had left us a little wired and a little drunk. It's as well neither of us had any life-or-death decisions to make just then. I wanted her to come up to my place so we could split the money, but she wanted to be downtown because she had a customer coming by early with a Giant Schnauzer, whatever the hell that is. We couldn't get a cab on West End Avenue, walked to Broadway, and ultimately kept the cab clear to the Village, where the driver was unable either to find Arbor Court on his own or to follow Carolyn's directions. We gave up finally and walked a couple of blocks. I hope he didn't squander his tip. Seventy years from now it might be valuable.

In Carolyn's apartment we got the Chagall litho out of my attaché case and held it up to the wall above the wicker chair. (That was another reason I'd accompanied her downtown, come to think of it. So that the picture could travel south in my case.) It looked good but the mat was the wrong color, so she decided to take it to a framer before hanging it. She poured herself a nightcap while I divvied up the cash. I gave her her share and she fanned the bills and whistled soundlessly at them. She said, "Not bad for a night's work, huh? I know it's not much for burglary, but it's different when your frame of reference is dog-grooming. You got any idea how many mutts I'd have to wash for this?"

"Lots."

"Bet your ass. Hey, I think you owe me a couple of bucks. Or are you charging me for the Chagall?"

"Of course not."

"Well, you gave me twelve hundred, and that's fifty dollars short of half. Not to be chintzy, but—"

"You're forgetting our expenses."

"What, cabfare? You paid one way and I paid coming back. What expenses?"

"Spinoza's *Ethics.*"

"I thought it came in with a load of books you bought by the yard. Or are you figuring on the basis of value instead of cost? That's fair, I don't care one way or the other, but—"

"I bought the book at Bartfield's on Fifty-seventh Street. It was a hundred dollars even. I didn't have to pay sales tax because I have a resale number."

She stared at me. "You paid a hundred dollars for that book?"

"Sure. Why? The price wasn't out of line."

"But you told Abel—"

"That I got it for next to nothing. I think he believed me, too. I also think it got us an extra five hundred bucks for the watch and the earrings. It put him in a generous frame of mind."

"Jesus," she said. "There's a lot I don't understand about this business."

"There's a lot nobody understands."

"Whoever heard of buying presents for a fence?"

"Whoever heard of a fence who quotes Spinoza?"

"That's a point. You sure you don't want a nightcap?"

"Positive."

"Did you know the nickel was worth that much?"

"I had a pretty good idea."

"You were so cool about it on the way up there. I had no idea it was worth a fortune."

"I just seemed cool."

"Yeah?" She cocked her head, studied me. "I'm glad we didn't take the ten grand apiece and say the hell with it. Why not take a gamble? It's not like I needed ten thousand dollars to get my kid brother an operation. How long do you think it'll take him to sell it?"

"There's no telling. He could move it tomorrow or sit on it for six months."

"But sooner or later the phone'll ring and we'll find out we just hit the Irish Sweepstakes."

"Something like that."

She stifled a yawn. "I thought I'd feel like celebrating tonight. But it's not really over yet, is it? It's probably a good thing. I don't think I've got the strength for a celebration. Besides, I'm sure to have a bitch of a sugar hangover in the morning."

"A sugar hangover?"

"All that pastry."

"You think it's the sugar that's going to give you a hangover?"

"What else?" She picked a cat off the couch, set him on the floor. "Sorry, fellow," she told him, "but it's bedtime for Mama."

"You sure you don't want the bed, Carolyn?"

"How are you supposed to fit on the couch? We'd have to fold you in half."

"It's just that I hate to chase you out of your own bed."

"Bern, we have this same argument every time you stay over. One of these days I'll actually let you have the couch and you'll never make the offer again."

So I took the bed and she took the couch, as usual, and I slept in my underwear and she in her Dr. Denton's. Ubi joined her on the couch. Archie, the Burmese, was restless at first, pacing the perimeters of the dark apartment like a rancher checking his fences. After a few circuits he threw himself onto the bed, flopped against me, and got the purring machine going. He was great at it, but then he's had all his life to practice.

Carolyn had had about three drinks to each of mine and they kept her from spending much time tossing and turning. In minutes her breathing announced that she was asleep, and in not too many more minutes she began emitting a ladylike snore.

I lay on my back, hands behind neck, eyes open, running the night's events through my mind. However long it took Abel to sell the nickel and whatever price we ultimately received for it, the Colcannon burglary was over and we were clear of it. As unpromising as it had been at first glance, when I'd seen we were not the first burglars to pay a call, things had worked out rather well. The loot was out of our hands, all but a rather anonymous minor Chagall litho which, given the chaos in the Colcannon carriage house, might never even get reported. And if it did, so what? It was one of a series of 250, and who'd come looking for it on Carolyn's wall anyway?

All the same, I put it in her closet when I awoke the next morning. It was around nine-thirty and she'd already fed herself and the cats and left for her Schnauzer appointment. I had a cup of coffee and a roll, tucked the litho away, let my attaché case keep it company rather than carry my burglar tools to work with me. The sun was shining, the air fresh and clean, and instead of contending with the subway I could walk to work. I could have run, for that matter—I had the shoes for it—but why spoil a beautiful morning? I strode along briskly, inhaling great lungfuls of air, swinging my arms at my sides. There was even a point when I caught myself whistling. I don't remember the tune.

I opened up around ten-fifteen and had my first customer twenty minutes later, a bearded pipe smoker who chose a couple volumes of English history. Then I sold a few things from the bargain table, and then trade slowed down enough for me to get back to the book I'd been reading yesterday. Old Spenser was still knocking himself out. This time he was doing bench presses, whatever they are, on a Universal machine. Whatever that is.

Two men in their forties walked in a little before eleven. They both wore dark suits and heavy shoes. One of them could have trimmed his sideburns a little higher. He was the one who walked to the back of the store while the other took an immediate and unconvincing interest in the poetry section.

I had Abel's thirteen hundred dollars in my wallet, plus the thousand dollars I always carry on a job in case I have to bribe somebody. I hoped they would settle for the money in the register. I hoped the bulge under the jacket of the sideburned chap wasn't really a gun, and that if it was he wouldn't decide to shoot me with it. I sent up an urgent brief prayer to Saint John of God, the patron saint of booksellers, a framed picture of whom old Mr. Litzauer had left hanging in the office. No point praying to Dismas now. I was bookselling, not burgling.

There was nothing I could do but wait for them to make a move, and I didn't have to do that for very long. They approached the counter, the one with the sideburns returning from the rear of the store, the other still clutching a volume of Robert W. Service's verses. I had a flash vision of one of them shooting me while the other recited "The Cremation of Sam McGee."

They reached the counter together. The Service fan said, "Rhodenbarr? Bernard Rhodenbarr?"

I didn't deny it.

"Better get your coat. Want to talk to you downtown."

"Thank God," I said.

Because, as you must have guessed and as I should have guessed, they weren't robbers after all. They were cops. And while cops may indeed rob you now and then, it's uncommon for them to do so at gunpoint. And gunpoint is something I prefer not to be at.

"He's glad to see us," said the sideburned chap.

The other nodded. "Probably a load off his mind."

"Sure. Probably up all night with guilt, aching to confess."

"I think you're right, Phil. Here's a guy, small-time burglar, he's in over his head. You look at his sheet, you can patch it together pretty good. He teamed up with somebody violent."

"I'm right with you, Dan. Bad companions."

"Do it every time. Now he's probably up to his kidneys in guilt and remorse. He can hand us the partner, make him the heavy, turn state's evidence and cop to a lesser charge. Good lawyer and the right attitude and what do you bet he's on the street in three years?"

"No bet, Phil. Three years, four at the outside. You want to close the store, Bernie? We'll just take a little ride downtown."

The fog lifted slowly. I'd been so relieved at not being robbed that it took a minute or two to realize I was being arrested, which is no pleasure in and of itself. They were talking to each other as if I weren't even in the room, but it was easy to see that I was the intended object of this merry little Phil-and-Dan patter. (Phil was the one with the sideburns, Dan the poetry lover.) According to their private script, I was supposed to be shaking in my Pumas even as they spoke.

Well, it was working.

"What's it all about?" I managed to ask.

"Some people would like to talk to you," Dan said.

48

"About what?"

"A little visit you paid last night to a house on Eighteenth Street," Phil said. "A little unannounced call."

Shit, I thought. How had they tagged us for Colcannon? My stomach turned with the beginnings of despair. It's particularly disheartening to be charged with a crime, I've found, when it's one you've committed. There's rather less opportunity for righteous indignation.

"So let's get going," Dan said. He set the book of poems on the counter. I found myself hoping his last name was McGrew, and that Phil would shoot him.

I'd just opened the store and now I had to close it. "Am I under arrest?" I asked.

"Do you want to be?"

"Not especially."

"Well, if you come with us voluntarily we won't have to arrest you."

That seemed fair enough. Phil helped me drag the bargain table inside, so I guessed that Dan ranked him. I locked the door and closed the gates, and while I was doing this they made the predictable jokes about a burglar locking up his own place, and how I didn't have to worry about forgetting my keys. Real sidesplitters, let me tell you.

Their car was a blue-and-white police cruiser. Phil drove while I sat in back with Dan. A couple blocks from the store I said, "What am I supposed to have done, anyway?"

"As if you didn't know."

"Right, as if I didn't. It happens I don't, so humor me. What's the charge?"

"He's cool now," Dan said to Phil. "Notice how the professional attitude comes into play? He was nervous before, but now he's cool as a pickle." He turned to me and said, "There's no charge. How can there be a charge? We didn't arrest you."

"If you arrested me, what would the charge have been?"

"Just hypothetically?"

"Okay."

"Burglary, first degree. And homicide, first degree." He shook his head. "You poor bastard," he said. "You never killed anybody before, did you?"

Six

Herbert and Wanda Colcannon had not stayed in Pennsylvania overnight after all. They had indeed driven out to Berks County, where they'd bred their beloved Bouvier to the chosen champion. Then they'd boarded Astrid overnight with the stud's owner, evidently a recommended procedure, and drove back to New York for dinner with business associates of Herbert's and an evening at the theater. After-theater drinks kept them out late, and they'd arrived home after midnight, intending to get a night's sleep and drive back to Pennsylvania first thing in the morning.

Instead, they had walked in on a burglary in progress. The burglars relieved Herbert of his cash and Wanda of the jewels she was wearing, then attempted to tie them up. When Herb protested, he got a punch in the mouth for his troubles. This provoked a voluble protest from Wanda, which earned her a couple of whacks on the head. Herb saw her fall and lie there motionless, and that was the last thing he saw, because that was when he got hit on the head himself.

When he came to he was tied up, and it took him a while to work his way loose. Wanda was also tied up, and she couldn't work her way loose because she was dead. She'd been hit on the head with something harder than her skull, and the fracture she'd sustained had proved fatal.

"That was your partner's doing," Sam Richler told me. He was the detective who seemed to be in charge of the case, and it was to him that Phil and Dan had turned me over upon arrival at police headquarters. "We know you're not violent by nature or habit, Rhodenbarr. You always used to work alone. What made you decide you needed a partner?"

"I don't have a partner," I said. "I don't even work alone anymore. I'm a legitimate businessman, I have a store, I sell books."

"Who was your partner? For Christ's sake, you don't want to protect him. He's the one put you in the soup. Look, I can see how it shapes. You retired, tried to make a go of it selling books"—he didn't believe this but was humoring me—"and this hard case talks you into trying one more job. Maybe he's got the place set up and he needs somebody with your talents to get around the locks. You figure you'll take one last job to keep you going while the store gets off its feet, and all of a sudden a woman's dead and your partner's off spending his money and you've got your head in the toilet. You know what you wanna do? You wanna pick your head up outta the bowl before somebody pulls the chain."

"That's a horrible image."

"You want a horrible image, I'll give you a horrible image." He opened a desk drawer, shuffled papers, came up with an eight-by-ten glossy. A woman, blond, wearing an evening gown, half sat against a wall in what looked to be the Colcannon living room. Her shoes were off, her ankles tied together, and her hands looked to be tied behind her back. The photo wasn't in color—which was just as well, thank you—but even in black and white one could see the discoloration right below the hairline where someone had struck her with something heavy. She looked horrible, all right; I had Carolyn's word that Wanda Colcannon was a beauty, but you couldn't prove it by this photograph.

"You didn't do that," Richler said. "Did you?"

"Do it? I can't even look at it."

"So give us the man who did. You'll get off light, Rhodenbarr. You might even walk with the right lawyer." Sure. "Thing is, we're certain to nail your partner anyway, with your help or without it. He'll run his mouth in a saloon and the right ear'll pick it up and we'll have him in a cell before it gets dark out. Or Colcannon'll find his mug shot in one of the books. Either way we get him. Only difference is if you help us you do your own self some good."

"It makes sense."

"That's just what it makes. Damn good sense. Plus you don't owe him a thing. Who got you in this mess, anyway?"

"That's a good question."

"So?"

"There's only one thing," I said.

"Oh?"

"I wasn't there. I never heard of anybody named Colcannon. I was nowhere near West Eighteenth Street. I gave up burglary when I bought the store."

"You're going to stick with that story?"

"I'm stuck with it. It happens to be the truth."

"We've got hard evidence that puts you right in that house."

"What evidence?"

"I'm not revealing that now. You'll find out when the time comes. And we've got Colcannon. I guess you didn't realize the woman was dead or you wouldn't have left him alive. Your accomplice wouldn't, anyway. We know he's the violent one. Maybe she was still alive when you left her. She could have died while he was unconscious. We don't have the medical examiner's report on that yet. But the thing is, see, we've got Colcannon and he can identify both you and your partner. So what's the point of sticking with your story?"

"It's the only story I've got."

"I suppose you've got an alibi to go with it?"

It would have been nice, but you can't have everything. "I sat home and watched television," I said. "Had a few beers, put my feet up."

"Just spent the whole night at home, huh?"

A little alarm went off. "The whole evening," I corrected. "After the eleven o'clock newscast I went out."

"And knocked over the Colcannon place."

"No. I had a late date."

"With anyone in particular?"

"With a woman."

"The kind of woman you can drop in on at eleven o'-clock."

"It was more like midnight by the time I met her."

"She got a name?"

"Uh-huh. But I'm not going to give it unless I have to. She's my alibi for the whole night, because I was with her from around midnight through breakfast this morning, and I'll use her if I don't have any choice, but not otherwise. She's separated from her husband and she's got a couple of young children and she doesn't need her name dragged into this. But that's where I was."

He frowned in thought. "You didn't get home last night," he said. "We know that much."

"I just told you."

"Yeah. We checked your apartment around four-thirty and left it staked out and you never showed up. But that's not enough to make me believe in your secret divorced lady."

"Not divorced. Separated."

"Uh-huh."

"And you don't have to believe in her. Just put me in the lineup and let Colcannon fail to identify me. Then I can go home."

"Who said anything about a lineup?"

"Nobody had to. You brought me here instead of the

54

precinct because this is where the mug shots are and you've got Colcannon looking through them. You haven't arrested me yet because he took a look at my picture and shook his head. Well, who knows, maybe I'm not photogenic, and it's worth letting him have a look at me in person, so that's why I'm here. Now you'll put me in a lineup and he'll say the same thing and I'll go back to my store and try to sell some books. It's hard to do much business when the store's closed."

"You really don't think he'll identify you."

"That's right."

"I don't get it," he said. He got to his feet. "Come on along," he said. "Let's take a walk."

We took a walk down the corridor and came to a door with frosted glass in the window and nothing written on it. "I'm not sure whether we want to bother with a lineup or not," he said, holding the door for me. "Whyntcha have a seat in here while I talk to some people and find out how they want to proceed?"

I went in and he closed the door. There was one chair in the room and it faced a large mirror, and Mrs. Rhodenbarr didn't raise no fools, so I knew right away why I was supposed to cool my heels in this particular little cubicle. What we were going to have was a one-man lineup, an unofficial lineup, and if it came out negative there wouldn't be a record of it to prejudice any case the State might decide to bring against one Bernard Grimes Rhodenbarr.

The mirror, I was bright enough to figure out, was of the one-way-glass variety. Herbert Franklin Colcannon would be positioned on the other side of it, where he could see me while I could not see him.

Fine with me.

In fact, I decided after a moment's reflection, it was more than fine with me, and the one thing I wanted to make sure of was that he got a good look at me, a good enough one to convince him once and for all that he had never seen me before. So I walked right up to the mirror, approaching it as if I thought it were indeed a mirror and nothing more. It was hard to repress the urge to make a face, but I squelched the impulse and adjusted the knot in my tie instead.

A funny thing about one-way glass. When you get close enough to it you can see through it. The vision you get is imperfect, because there's still a mirror effect and you get a sort of double image like a piece of twice-exposed photographic film, seeing what's in front of you and what's behind you at the same time. What I saw for a while was an empty room, and then I saw Richler bring in a man in a gray suit with a bandage on his head and a lot of swelling and discoloration around it.

He approached the mirror and stared at me, and I stared right back at him. It took an enormous effort of will to avoid winking or extending my tongue or rolling my eyes or doing something similarly harebrained. Instead I took my time looking him over.

He wasn't terribly impressive. He was an inch or two below medium height and he looked to be about fifty-five. An oval face, slate-gray hair, a small clipped mustache with some white in with the gray. A snub nose, a small mouth. Eyes an indeterminate color somewhere between brown and green. If you saw him you'd guess banker first, tax lawyer second. He didn't particularly look like a man who'd just lost a glamorous wife and a $500,000 coin, but then he didn't look like a man who'd had either of them in the first place.

He looked at me and I looked at him, and he shook his head from side to side, solemn as an owl.

I don't think I smiled, not just then, but when he turned at Richler's touch and followed the detective out of the room I grinned like a Hallowe'en pumpkin. When Richler walked in a few minutes later I was sitting in the chair cleaning my fingernails with the blunt end of a toothpick. I looked up brightly and asked him if they were going to put me in a lineup.

"You're cute as a button," he said.

"Pardon me?"

"Straightening your goddamn tie. No, there's not going to be a lineup, Rhodenbarr. You can go home now."

"The police realize their mistake?"

"I don't think we made one. I think you pulled that burglary last night. I think you were upstairs goosing the wall safe while your partners were roughing up the Colcannons. That way he never got a look at you, and you think that's gonna save your neck. It's not. We'll still get your pals, and we've still got evidence against you, and you'll wind up taking twice the fall you'd take if you cooperated. But you're a wiseass and it's your funeral."

"I'm just a used-book dealer."

"Sure you are. What you can do right now is get the hell out of here. You're not bright enough to recognize it when someone's trying to give you a break. If you wake up in a couple of hours, give me a call. But you don't want to wait too long. If we get one of your partners first, he'll be the one turning state's evidence and what'll we need with you? You'll be the one doing the long time, and you weren't even there when the woman got killed, and what sense does that make? You sure you still don't want to come clean?"

"I already came clean."

"Yeah, sure. Get out, Rhodenbarr."

I was on my way out of the building when I heard a familiar voice speak my name. "If it ain't Bernie Rhodenbarr. Hang around No. 1 Police Plaza and you never know who you'll run into."

"Hello, Ray."

"Hello yourself, Bernie." Ray Kirschmann gave me a lopsided grin. His suit didn't fit him very well, but then his suits never do. You'd think with all the shakedown money he takes he could afford to dress better. "Beautiful mornin', huh, Bern?"

"Beautiful."

"Except it's past noon now. An' I see I won a little bet I made with myself. They're lettin' you go home."

"You know about it?"

"Sure. The Colcannon thing. I knew you didn't do it. When did you ever work with a partner? And when did you ever pull anything violent. Except"—and he looked reproachful—"for the time you hit me and knocked me down. You remember that, Bern?"

"I panicked, Ray."

"I remember it well."

"And I wasn't trying to hurt you. I was just trying to get away."

"Uh-huh. They still figure you're it, you know. Richler's got enough to hold you on. He thinks he'll have a stronger case in the long run if he doesn't slap you in a cell just yet."

We were standing on the pavement outside the red-brick structure, looking across the plaza at the central arch of the Municipal Building. Ray cupped his hands to light a cigarette, inhaled, coughed, took another drag. "Beautiful day," he said. "Just gorgeous."

"Why do they think I was involved in the Colcannon burglary?"

"Your M.O., Bern."

"You've got to be kidding. When did I ever turn a place upside down and leave a mess? When did I ever hurt anybody, or do anything but run like a thief if the owners came home while I was working? When did I ever get into a place by smashing a skylight? How does all that add up to my *modus operandi?*"

"They figure your partners were sloppy and violent. But they've got evidence that fits you like a glove."

"What do you mean?"

"Here's what I mean." He reached into his jacket pocket

58

and came up with something that he dangled from thumb and forefinger. It was a Playtex Living Glove, but he held it as if it had died.

The palm had been cut out of it.

"That's your evidence?"

"Their evidence, not mine. It's on your sheet, Bern. 'Wears rubber gloves with palms excised.' I like that word, excised. That means you cut the palms out but they can't come right out and say so, you know?"

"For God's sake," I said. "Where did they find this?"

"Right outside of Colcannon's house. There's a garden there and that's where it was."

"Can I see it?"

"It's evidence."

"So was the glass slipper," I said, taking the glove from him, trying to force my hand into it. "And I must be one of Cinderella's ugly sisters because this thing doesn't fit. It doesn't even come close to fitting. They make these things in sizes, Ray, and this one's just not my size."

He took a close look. "You know somethin'? I think you're right."

I gave the glove back to him. "Take care of this. You might even tell them the glove's the wrong size. They can start looking around for a klutzy burglar with very small hands."

"I'll spread the word. You headin' back to the store now? I'll give you a ride."

"All part of the service?"

"Just that it's on my way. What the hell."

This time I got a ride in an unmarked car. We made small talk about the Mets' new third baseman, a possible garbage strike, and a shakeup in the Queens District Attorney's office. Crooks and cops always have plenty of things to talk about once they can get past the basic adversary nature of their relationship. The two classes actually have more in common than either of us would like to admit. Phil and Dan, who couldn't have looked more like cops unless they'd been in uniform, had looked like robbers to me when they came into my store.

Ray dropped me right in front of Barnegat Books, told me to take care, gave me a slow wink, and drove off. I started to open up, looked to see if he was gone, then said to hell with it and refastened the locks I'd opened. I had to do a few things that were more important than selling books.

I hadn't been part of the gang of burglars who'd killed Wanda Colcannon. Her husband hadn't merely failed to identify me. He'd given them a firm negative identification. And if the rubber glove was all they had, their evidence was a joke.

But Richler still thought I was involved.

And something funny, something I'd realized at the very end of the ride back to the store. Ray Kirschmann thought so, too.

Seven

Carolyn and I usually have lunch together. Mondays and Wednesdays I pick up something and we eat at the Poodle Factory. Tuesdays and Thursdays she brings our lunch to the bookstore. Fridays we generally go someplace ethnic and inexpensive and toss a coin for the check. All of this, of course, is subject to change if anything comes up, and Carolyn must have gathered that something had. It was a Wednesday, so when I'd failed to turn up around noon she'd evidently gone somewhere herself. The Poodle Factory was closed, with a cardboard sign hanging on the back of the door. *"Back At,"* the sign said, and beneath it the movable clock hands pointed to one-thirty.

I looked in at the coffee shop on the corner of Broadway but didn't see her. There was a pay phone on the wall at the back but it looked a little too exposed. I walked north a block and checked the felafel place. She wasn't there, either, but their pay phone was a little more private. I ordered a cup of coffee and a hommos sandwich. I wasn't especially hungry but I hadn't had anything since my roll for breakfast and figured I probably ought to eat. I ate most of my sandwich, drank all of my coffee, and made sure I got some dimes in my change.

The first call I made was to Abel Crowe. The *Post* was on the street by now, and I didn't have to look at it to know that Wanda Colcannon would be spread all over page three. Her murder might even get the front page, unless something more urgent displaced it, like a projected invasion of killer bees from South America. (Once, during the Son of Sam foofaraw, they'd given the entire front page to a photo of David Berkowitz asleep in his cell. "SAM SLEEPS!" the headline shrieked.)

At any rate, the murder was general knowledge by now and one medium or another was sure to call it to Abel's attention. Any stolen object with a six-figure price tag is hot enough to blister the skin, but homicide always turns up the heat, and Abel would not be happy. Nor could I make him happy, but I could at least assure him that we were burglars, not murderers.

I let the phone ring an even dozen times. When my dime came back I stood there for a minute, then tried the number again. One sometimes misdials, and telephone-company equipment sometimes misbehaves.

No answer. I'd dialed his number from memory and there was no directory handy to confirm my recollection, so I let Information check it for me. I'd remembered correctly, but to be on the safe side I dialed it yet again, and when there was still no answer I gave up. Maybe he was already out selling the coin. Maybe he was at his favorite bakery on West Seventy-second Street, buying up everything in sight. Maybe he was napping with the phone's bell muffled, or soaking in the tub, or tempting muggers in Riverside Park.

I dialed 411 again and let them look up another number for me. Narrowback Gallery, on West Broadway in SoHo. The phone rang four times, just long enough for me to decide I wasn't destined to reach anybody this afternoon, and then

Denise Raphaelson answered, her voice scratchy from the cigarettes she chain-smoked.

"Hi," I said. "Are we set for dinner tonight?"

"Bernie?"

"Uh-huh."

There was a pause. "I'm a little confused," she said finally. "I've been painting my brains out and I think the fumes are starting to get to me. Did we have a dinner date for tonight?"

"Well, yeah. It was sort of mentioned casually. Too casually, I guess, if it slipped your mind."

"I should write these things down," she said, "but I never do. I'm sorry, Bernie."

"You made other plans."

"I did? I don't think I did. Of course if I could forget a dinner date with you, I could forget other things at least as easily. For all I know I'm throwing a party tonight. Truman and Gore are coming, and Hilton wanted a quick look at my latest work before he does his piece for the Sunday *Times*, and Andy said he'd bring Marlene if she's in town. What do you suppose it's like being one of those people that people know who you are without hearing your last name? I bet if I was Jackie I'd still have to show ID to cash a check at D'Agostino's."

Telephonic whimsy is her specialty. We'd first met over the phone when I was trying to find an artist without knowing anything about him but his last name. She'd told me how to manage that, and one thing had led to another, as it so often does. We have since seen each other now and again, and if it's all remained very casual and on the surface, that's not the worst thing that can be said of what one has learned to call interpersonal relationships.

"What I should have done," she said now, "is fake it. When you asked if we were set for dinner tonight I should have said yes and let it go at that. It's a shame I don't take drugs. Then I could blame this mental sluggishness on the joint I'd just smoked. Would you believe paint fumes?"

"Sure."

"Because I *am* free for dinner, and just because I don't seem to recall our date shouldn't prevent me from keeping it. Did we make plans to meet someplace?"

"Not yet."

"Should we?"

"Why don't I drop by your place around seven-thirty?"

"Why don't you?"

"I think I will."

"I think you should. Shall I cook something?"

"We'll go out."

"This is sounding better and better. Maybe I'll have this painting finished and you can look at it. Maybe I won't and you can't. 'Bernie at 7:30.' I've written it down. I can't possibly forget now."

"I have faith in you, Denise."

"Shall I wear anything in particular?"

"Just a smock and a smile."

"Ta."

I tried Abel again, twelve rings and out. By then it was one-thirty. I hiked back to the Poodle Factory and caught Carolyn between appointments. "There you are," she said. "When you didn't show I went looking for you, and when I saw your store was closed I figured you'd just ducked out to pick up lunoh, so I came back here and waited, and when you still didn't show I said the hell with it and went out and ate."

"Not at the coffee shop," I said, "and not at Mamoun's."

"I went and had some curry. I figured some really hot food would counteract the sugar from last night. God, what a morning!"

"Bad?"

"My head felt like the soccer ball from Pélé's last game.

You have any idea what it's like to face a Giant Schnauzer on top of a sugar hangover?"

"No."

"Count your lucky stars. The coffee shop and Mamoun's —what did you do, go out looking for me?"

"Sort of."

"Any particular reason?"

I hated to ruin her day, but what else could I do? "Just wanted to tell you you were missing a glove," I said. "Of the rubber variety, and with the palm cut out."

"Son of a bitch."

"You weren't going to say that, remember? You were going to switch to 'child of a dog' because 'son of a bitch' is sexist."

"Shit. I saw the glove was missing last night when I checked my pockets. I threw away the one but the other was gone. I thought it over and decided not to tell you. How'd you find out? What did you do, go through my garbage?"

"I always go through your garbage. It started out as a perversion and now it's a hobby."

"That's the way it always works."

"I didn't go through your garbage. You dropped it in the garden, in case you were wondering."

"I did? Jesus, they ought to put me away. How do you know this? You didn't go back there, did you? No, of course you didn't."

"No. Somebody showed me the glove."

"Who would—" Light dawned and her face fell. "Oh, no," she said. "Cops."

"Right."

"You got arrested."

"Not officially."

"What happened?"

"They let me go. My hands are bigger than yours. The glove didn't fit. And Herbert Colcannon didn't recognize me."

"Why would he recognize you? He never met you."

"Right. I'll bet you didn't read the paper at lunch."

"I read the *Times* this morning. Why?"

"It's complicated," I said, "but it's important. You'd better hear the whole thing."

Her phone rang a couple of times while I was going through it. She switched on the answering machine and let her callers leave messages if they wanted. We were interrupted once by a sad-eyed man wearing an obvious toupee who wanted to inquire about services and rates. If his pet resembled him, he probably had a basset hound.

When I was finished Carolyn just sat there shaking her head. "I don't know what to say," she said. "I'm sorry about the glove, Bern. I feel rotten about it."

"These things happen."

"I thought I'd be a help and look what I did. I might as well have left a trail of bread crumbs."

"The birds would have eaten them."

"Yeah. I can't believe she's dead. Wanda Flanders Colcannon. I can't believe it."

"You'd believe it if you saw the picture."

She shuddered, made a face. "Burglary's fun," she said. "But murder—"

"I know."

"I don't understand how it happened. The other burglars, the slobs, got there *before* we did."

"Right."

"And turned the place upside down and stole God knows what and left."

"Right."

"And then came back? Why? Don't tell me it's true about criminals returning to the scene of the crime?"

"Only to commit another crime. Remember, we didn't know the Colcannons were planning to leave Astrid. We thought they were staying overnight."

"I'm sorry about that, too."

"Don't be. You couldn't know otherwise. The point is, the other burglars probably made the same assumption. Suppose they grabbed up everything they could, took off over the rooftops, then decided they'd like to have another shot at the wall safe. They had time to pick up a torch or a drill. They might not have brought the right equipment the first time because they might not even have known about the safe, but if they had time to pick up a torch and all night to work on the safe, why not give it the old college try?"

"And then the Colcannons came home right in the middle of it?"

"Evidently."

"If they did, wouldn't the burglars make them give them the combination of the safe?"

"Probably. Unless they'd already opened it."

"If they had, why would they still be hanging around?"

"They wouldn't. But the Colcannons could have walked in the door just as the burglars were on their way out."

"Wouldn't they leave the way they came? Through the skylight?"

"You're right," I said. I frowned. "Anyway, there's a third possibility. There could have been a third set of burglars."

"A third set? How many people knew that damned dog was going to Pennsylvania to get laid?"

"Maybe these last burglars weren't real burglars," I suggested. "Maybe they were kids or junkies on the prowl, just roaming across the rooftops to see what they turned up. They'd notice the broken skylight and drop in for a look around. There were still plenty of things there to steal if you were an amateur on the prowl. Remember the radio? That would bring the price of a bag of heroin."

"There was at least one television set. Plus some stereo components on the second floor."

"See what I mean? Loads of goodies for a thief with low

standards. But there wasn't a lot of money, and sometimes amateur thieves take that sort of thing personally. You know how muggers sometimes beat up people who don't have any cash on them?"

"I've heard of that."

"Well, there's a class of burglars who get the same sort of resentment. I can imagine a couple of punks dropping in through the broken skylight, picking up a radio and a portable TV, then deciding to hang around until the householders come home so they can rob them of their cash." I followed that train of thought for a minute, then dropped it and shrugged. "It doesn't really matter. I may have to spend the next week looking over my shoulder for cops, but basically we're in the clear. The thing is, they're going to find the guys who did it. There'll be a lot of heat with her murdered, and Richler was right. He said somebody would blab at a bar and somebody else would overhear him. That's what usually happens and it's how most crimes get solved."

"And you think we're all right?"

"Sure. Colcannon can identify the men who killed his wife. We've already established that he can't identify me. All they've got that leads to me is a rubber glove, and if the glove doesn't fit, how can I wear it? If one of us had to drop a glove, I'm damned glad it was you."

"I wish that made me feel better."

"You've got to look on the bright side. Another thing to be glad of is that Colcannon wasn't killed. If they had known Wanda was dead they probably would have killed him, too, and then he wouldn't have been around to get me off the hook."

"I didn't think of that."

"I did." I lifted the phone from her desk. "Anyway, I'd better call Abel."

"Why?"

"To tell him we didn't kill anybody."

"He already knows that, doesn't he? It's a shame neither of us bothered to read the *Post,* but won't it tell what time she was killed?"

"Probably."

"Well, it was around 11:30 when we got to Abel's. I remember it was 12:07 when he checked the Piaget watch against yours. And it was after midnight when the Colcannons walked in on the burglars, so how could Abel think we did it?"

"My God," I said. "He's our alibi."

"Sure."

"I hope to God we never have to use him. Imagine trying to beat a burglary charge by insisting you were spending the time with a fence, trying to sell the things you'd already lifted from the burglary victim."

"When you put it that way, it does sound bizarre."

"I know." I began dialing. "I'll call him anyway and put him in the picture. He may not have noticed the timing and assume we killed that woman, and I wouldn't want that."

"Would he refuse to handle the coin?"

"Why?"

"If we were killers—"

The phone was ringing. I let it ring. "Abel's a fence," I said. "Not a judge. Anyway, we didn't do it and I can make him believe it. If he'd ever answer his goddamned phone."

I hung up. Carolyn frowned to herself for a moment, then said, "It's just business as usual, isn't it? Wanda's dead but nothing's changed. Abel will sell the coin in a few days or a few months and we'll get our share, same as if nothing ever happened to her."

"That's right."

"It seems wrong. I don't know why."

"We didn't kill her, Carolyn."

"I know that."

"We didn't do anything to cause her death."

"I know that, too. It was some other guys and they had

no connection with us. I understand all that, Bern. I just feel funny, that's all. What do you think we'll get?"

"Huh?"

"For the coin."

"Oh. I don't know."

"How will we know what price he sells it for?"

"He'll tell us."

"What I mean is he won't cheat us, will he?"

"Abel? He might."

"Really?"

"Well, the man's a receiver of stolen goods," I said. "I imagine he's told a lie or two in the course of a long life. I don't suppose he'd draw the line at telling another. And it's the easiest sort of a lie because there's no way for us to know about it."

"Then how can we trust him?"

"In a sense I don't suppose we can. Not to be perfectly honest, anyway. If he got lucky and peddled the V-Nickel for half a million dollars, say, I'd guess he might tell us he got two hundred thousand dollars for it. We'd get half of that, and I suppose he'd have cheated us out of a bundle if that happened, but would we really have a complaint? It would be hard for me to work up much indignation if my end of a night's work came to fifty thousand dollars."

"Suppose he tells us he sold it for fifty thousand? Then what?"

"Then he'll probably be telling the truth. My guess is that he'd be most likely to cheat us if the coin sells high and most likely to be completely honest if the selling price is low. And we can be sure that our end won't drop below seventeen thousand five hundred, because he offered us that much for cash on delivery, so he'll make sure we get more than that if we have to wait for our money. Unless the coin turns out to be a counterfeit, in which case all bets are off."

"Is that a possibility?"

"No. It's a genuine coin. My prediction is that you and I will wind up dividing fifty thousand dollars."

"Jesus. And all we have to do is sit around and wait for it?"

"Right. What was it the German officer used to say to POWs in the war movies? 'My friend, for you ze var is over.' I think I'll celebrate the end of the war by opening the store for a couple of hours. You doing anything special tonight?"

"I'll probably bounce around the bars eventually. Why? Want to have dinner?"

"Can't. I've got a date."

"Anybody I know?"

"Denise."

"The painter? The one who doesn't shut up?"

"She has a ready wit and a self-deprecatory sense of humor."

"If you say so, Bern."

"Do I criticize your taste in women?"

"Sometimes."

"Hardly ever," I said. I got up. "I'm going to sell some books. I'll call you later if I hear anything. Have a good time at the dyke bars."

"I intend to," she said. "Give my love to Denise."

Eight

Denise Raphaelson is long-legged and slender, although Carolyn insists on describing her as gawky and bony. Her hair is dark brown and curly and worn medium-long, her complexion fair with a dusting of unobtrusive freckles. Her blue-gray eyes are artist's eyes, always measuring and assessing and seeing the world as a series of framed rectangles.

There was no end of rectangles, albeit unframed, on the walls of Narrowback Gallery, where she lived and worked. It's on the third floor of a loft building on West Broadway between Grand and Broome, and its name derived from the loft's unusual shape, narrow at the back and wider at the front. Denise subsequently discovered that *narrowback* is a term of contempt applied by native Irish to those kinsmen of theirs who have emigrated to America. No one has yet satisfactorily explained the term to her, although speculation on the subject has sparked any number of drunken conversations at the Broome Street Bar.

I looked at a couple of paintings she'd done since I was last at the loft, including the one she'd been working on that day. I exchanged a few sentences with Jared, her twelve-year-old genius son, and gave him the stack of paperback science fiction I'd been setting aside for him. (I don't handle paperbacks in the store, wholesaling the ones that come in to a store that sells nothing else.) He seemed happy with what I'd brought, especially an early Chip Delaney novel that he'd been wanting to read, and we had the sort of stilted conversation one has with the precocious and overly hip child of a woman with whom one occasionally beds down.

I'd gone home to shave and change clothes before trekking down to SoHo. I had my Weejuns on my feet again and was comfortably casual in Levi's and a flannel shirt. Denise was wearing a lime turtleneck and a pair of those forty-dollar jeans with an over-the-hill debutante's autograph on a rear pocket. Remember when clothes had their labels on the inside?

We had a glass of wine each at the gallery, then moved on to an Ethiopian place in Tribeca where you bring your own wine and eat unpronounceable dishes at your peril. We brought a rosé to see if it really does go with anything, and it did, but not terribly well. Our dishes, hers made with chicken and mine with lamb, were identically sauced and hot enough to blister paint. They came with a disc of spongy bread the size of a small pizza, and we tore off hunks of this gooey muck and used it to scoop up mouthfuls of the hot stuff. In the name of ethnic authenticity, a whole lot of New Yorkers are relearning the table manners of messy children.

When we got out of there—and not a moment too soon— we walked around for a while and wound up listening to a jazz trio on Wooster Street. We had a couple of Scotches there and Denise worked her way through a pack of Virginia Slims. I tried Abel once or twice, and then we walked north a ways and caught Lance Hayward's ten o'clock set at the Village Corner. Denise knows him, so we chatted with him after the set and it turned out there was another pianist we simply had to hear at a new club in my neighborhood. I dialed Abel's number again and we had a quick drink with

Lance—we were drinking stingers by this time—before grabbing a cab uptown.

The new club was on Columbus Avenue in the low eighties and the piano player was a young black kid who kept reminding me of a Lennie Tristano record I hadn't listened to in years. We got out of there when the set ended and cabbed to my place, where I dug out the record in question and put it on. We had a nightcap and threw our clothes on the floor and dived into bed.

I did not find her to be gawky and bony. I found her to be warm and soft and quick and eager, and the music's eccentric harmonies and offbeat rhythm didn't interfere with the pleasure we took with one another. If anything, it gave a nice brittly atonal edge to our lovemaking.

The tone arm had just dropped to begin replaying the record for the third time when she yawned and stretched and reached for the inevitable cigarette. She got it lit and said something about going home.

"Stay over," I suggested.

"I didn't say anything to Jared. I figured we'd wind up at my place."

"And if you're not there when he wakes up?"

"He'll figure I'm here, which is cool, but if I'd known I would have called him earlier. I'd call now but I don't want to wake him."

I thought of trying Abel again but it would have involved moving.

"I think I *will* stay," she said, after a moment's reflection. "Mind if I change the record?"

"Not at all. Put on a stack."

She crouched at the record rack, her bare behind tilted charmingly in my direction. Bony? Gawky? Pfui.

When she came back to bed I slipped an arm around her and told her I was glad she was staying.

"Me too," she said.

"You said earlier that you went to the movies last night."

"Right. I took the kid and we saw the new Woody Allen picture."

"And you loved it but he thought it was superficial."

"Yeah, the little wiseass."

"Do anything afterwards?"

She shifted around, glanced up at me. "A little dancing," she said, "but no fooling around. What do you mean?"

"You went to the movies and then you and Jared went home and you stayed there?"

"Right. Except that we stopped on the way home for frozen yogurt. Why?"

"When did he go to sleep?"

"Around eleven, maybe a little later."

"It won't come up," I said, "but if it does, I was over at your place last night. I got there around midnight after the kid went to bed and left first thing in the morning."

"I see."

"What do you see?"

She sat up, lit another Virginia Slim. "I see why you called me this afternoon."

"You do like hell."

"Oh? You burgled somebody last night and you need an alibi, so Denise is elected. I thought you gave up stealing, you swore you gave up stealing, but what does it mean when a thief takes an oath? Good old Denise. Take her out for a meal, pour a few drinks into her, hit a few jazz clubs, then throw her a friendly fuck—"

"Cut it out."

"Why should I? Isn't that about how it goes?"

Jesus, why had I brought it up? Well enough seems to be the one thing I'm incapable of leaving alone.

I said, "You're wrong, but maybe you're too mad to listen to an explanation. I called you because we had a date for tonight." The best defense is a good offense, isn't it? "Don't blame me for your bad memory. I can't help that."

"I didn't—"

"I *did* give up burglary, and I'm not exactly in trouble, but someone committed a crime last night and used the type of gloves I used to use, and the police found one on the scene and think I'm involved. And I don't happen to have an alibi because I happened to spend the night alone, because who knew I was going to *need* an alibi? When you don't do anything criminal you don't bother to arrange an alibi in advance."

"And you just sat home in front of the television set?"

"As a matter of fact I was reading Spinoza."

"I don't suppose anyone would make that up. Except you might." She fixed those artist's eyes on me. "I don't know how much of your word to take. Where was the burglary? Oh, wait a minute. It wasn't the one I read about in the paper? That poor woman in Chelsea?"

"That's the one."

"You didn't do that, did you, Bernie?" Her eyes probed mine for a long moment. Then she took one of my hands in both of hers and looked at my fingers. "No," she said, more to herself than to me. "You're very gentle. You couldn't kill someone."

"Of course I couldn't."

"I believe you. You said they found a glove? Does that mean you're in trouble?"

"Probably not. They'll probably catch the guys who did it within a couple of days. But in the meantime I figured it wouldn't hurt to have someone back up my story, in case anybody ever leans on it."

She asked what story I'd told them and I repeated my conversation with Richler.

"You didn't tell them my name," she said. "That's good. So I won't come into it unless they give you more trouble and you need a backup."

"That's right."

"Why didn't you just tell them the truth? That you were home watching TV?"

"I tend to lie to cops."

"Oh?"

"Old habits die hard."

"I guess." She leaned over to stub out her cigarette in the ashtray on the bedside table. In that position the curve of her pendant breast was particularly appealing, and I reached out a hand and stroked her. Bony? Gawky?

"I feel manipulated," she said lazily. "And as though I've been lied to a little."

"Maybe a very little," I conceded.

"Well, nobody's perfect."

"That's the prevailing opinion, anyway."

"And I'm a little sleepy and the least bit horny, and isn't Duke Ellington divine? Thief that you are, why don't you steal a little kiss?"

"God knows where that might lead."

"He's not the only one."

Nine

I woke up around seven to let her out. I have several locks on the door in addition to the police lock, and she was having a hell of a time getting them all lined up. I unlocked everything and told her I'd call her, and she said that would be nice, and we gave each other one of those near-miss kisses you exchange when one or more of you has not recently employed a toothbrush.

I locked up after her and went to the bathroom, where I employed a toothbrush and swallowed a couple of aspirin. I thought about breakfast, thought better of it, and decided to lie down for a minute to give the aspirins a chance to work.

Next thing I knew, someone was pummeling my door. I thought first that it was Denise, come to retrieve something. But it didn't sound like her. Nor did it sound like little Mrs. Hesch, my one friend in that soulless building. Mrs. Hesch drops by now and again to pour me a cup of great coffee and bitch about the building management's failure to keep the washers and dryers in good repair. But Mrs. Hesch is a little bird of a woman, not much given to pounding on one's door.

More knocking. I had my feet on the floor now and some

of the fog was starting to lift from my brain. It was cops, of course, as I realized as soon as I was awake enough to be capable of things like realization. Nobody else knocks like that, as if you should have been expecting them and ought to have met them at the door.

I went to the door and asked who it was. "Well, it ain't Santy Claus," said a recognizable voice. "Open up, Bern."

"Oh, hell."

"What kind of attitude is that?"

"You picked a bad time," I said. "Why don't I meet you in the lobby in say five minutes?"

"Why don't you open the door in say ten seconds?"

"The thing is," I said, "I'm not dressed."

"So?"

"Give me a minute."

What time was it, anyway? I found my watch and learned it was a few minutes past nine, which meant I was going to be late opening up the store. I might miss selling a few three-for-a-buck books as a result, and while that's hard to take seriously when you've just stolen something with a six-figure price tag, standards must be maintained.

I got into some clothes, splashed a handful of cold water on my face, and opened a window to air the place out a little. Then I unlocked all my locks for the second time that morning, and Ray Kirschmann shook his head at them as he lumbered across my threshold.

"Look at that," he said. "Figure you got enough security devices there, Bern?"

Security devices, yet. Anybody but a cop would have called the damn things locks. "They say you can't be too careful," I said.

"That's what they say, all right. Police lock's new, isn't it? You gettin' paranoid in your old age?"

"Well, we've had a rash of burglaries in the neighborhood. Four or five right in this building."

"Even with the doorman on the job?"

"He's not exactly the Secret Service," I said. "Incidentally, I must not have heard him ring to announce you."

"I sort of told him not to take the trouble, Bern. I said I'd just make things easy and go straight up."

"Did you tell him you were Santa Claus?"

"Why would I do that?"

"Because that's who's going to have to take care of him at Christmas. I'm not even putting coal in his stocking."

"Funny. What did you have, company last night?"

"You didn't get that from the doorman."

He looked pleased. "I'm a detective," he said. "What I did, I detected it. Well, look around, Bern. Ashtray full of cigarette butts and you don't smoke. Two glasses, one on each of the bedside tables. If she's hidin' in the bathroom, tell her to come join the party."

"She already went home, but I'm sure she'd appreciate the invitation."

"She's not here?"

"No. You missed her by a couple hours."

"Well, thank God for small favors."

"Huh?"

"Now I can use your bathroom."

When he emerged from it I was sipping a glass of orange juice and feeling more alert, if not altogether on top of things. "You just dropped in to use the john," I said. "Right?"

"You kiddin', Bern? I came by to see you. We don't see each other that often."

"I know. It's been ages."

"It seems I only see you when somebody gets killed. You had overnight company, huh? That's not bad, two nights in a row."

"The other night I was at her place."

"Same lady, huh?"

"That's right."

"Handy."

"Ray, it's always wonderful to see you," I said, "but I overslept and I'm late getting to the store as it is, and—"

"Business comes first, right?"

"Something like that."

"Sure, I know how it is, Bern. I wouldn't be here myself if it wasn't business. Who's got the time for social calls, right?"

"Right."

"So I guess you got yourself an alibi for last night. The little lady who smoked all the cigarettes."

"She's not so little. There are those who would call her gawky. And I already told Richler all that. I'll give her name if I absolutely have to, if I'm charged and booked, but until then—"

"That's the night before last, Bern. The Colcannon job, I'm talkin' about last night."

"What about last night?"

"Tell me about it. Matter of fact, take it from when I dropped you off at the store yesterday around noon. Run it down for me."

"What's last night got to do with anything?"

"You first, Bern."

He listened attentively, and I could almost see wheels turning behind his forehead. Just because his integrity's for sale doesn't change the fact that Ray Kirschmann's a pretty good cop. It is not for nothing that he is known as the best cop money can buy.

When I was finished he frowned, sucked at his teeth, clucked his tongue, yawned, and allowed as to how my alibi sounded pretty good.

"It's not an alibi," I said. "It's what I did yesterday. An alibi's when something happened and you have to prove you didn't do it."

"Right."

"What happened?"

"Friend of yours got hisself killed. Least he used to be a friend of yours. Before you went straight and gave up burgling for books."

I felt a chill. He could have meant anyone but I knew without a moment's doubt just who it was that he was talking about.

"A top fence. What the papers'll call a notorious receiver of stolen goods, except they better say *alleged* because he never took a fall for it. Somebody got into his apartment yesterday and beat him to death."

Ten

"You're not a suspect," Ray assured me. "Nobody on the case even gave a thought to you. Then I went in this morning and I got the word on Crowe and the first person I thought of was you. 'Here I just saw my old friend Bernie Rhoden-barr yesterday,' I said to myself, 'and here's an old friend of his that turns up murdered, and one thing Crowe and the Colcannon woman got in common is they both died from a beatin'.' So what I thought is you might know somethin'. What do you know, Bern?"

"Nothing."

"Yeah. But what do you know besides that?"

We were in the same car we'd ridden in a day ago, and once again he was driving me to my store. I told him I hadn't seen Abel Crowe since a friend and I had watched the fire-works from his living-room window almost a year ago.

"Yeah, that's some view," he said. "I dropped by on my way to your place just to see what I could see. What I could see was half of Jersey from the living-room window. That's where they found the body, over by the window, all crum-pled in a heap. You never saw him since the Fourth of July?"

"We may have talked a few times on the phone, but not recently. And I haven't seen him since last July."

"Yeah. What happened yesterday, a neighbor rang his bell around six, six-thirty in the afternoon. When he didn't answer she got concerned and checked with the doorman, and he didn't remember Crowe leavin' the buildin'. An old man like that, you worry about his heart or maybe he had a fall, things like that. The guy was seventy-one."

"I didn't realize he was that old."

"Yeah, seventy-one. So the doorman went upstairs, or more likely he sent somebody, the elevator operator or a porter or somebody, and they tried the door. But that didn't do 'em any good because he had police locks like you got on your door. A different model, the kind with the bolt that slides across."

"I know."

"Oh, yeah? You remember his locks clear from last July?"

"Now that you mention it I do. The business I was in, you tend to pay attention to locks."

"I'll bet you do. What they did, they banged on the door and tried to get an answer, and then they called the precinct and a patrolman was sent up, and what could he do? He tried to force the door and you can't with a lock like that, and finally someone got the bright idea to call a locksmith, and by the time they found someone who would come and he finally got there and managed to open the lock it must have been close to ten o'clock."

Indeed it must have. It wasn't too much earlier than that when I last tried Abel's number, and if they'd gotten in earlier some cop would have answered Abel's telephone.

"They almost expected to find the old man lyin' dead there," he went on. "What they didn't expect was to find him murdered."

"There's no question it was murder?"

"No question at all. The Medical Examiner on the scene said so, although you didn't have to be a doctor to see it. It wasn't one blow. Somebody hit him a lot of times in the face and over the head."

"God."

"Time of death's a guess at this stage, but the ballpark figure is early afternoon yesterday. So you could have raced up there after I dropped you at the store, killed the old man, then raced back down to open up for business. Just a little lunch-hour homicide. Except that's not your style an' we both know it, plus I got a look at your face when I told you about Crowe bein' dead, Bern, and you were learnin' it for the first time."

We caught a light at Thirty-seventh Street and he braked the car. "The thing is," he said, "it's a coincidence, isn't it? Colcannon and now this, both hit on the head and both dead and not twenty-four hours apart. More like twelve hours."

"Was Crowe's apartment robbed?"

"It wasn't taken apart. If anybody stole anything it didn't show. I got there long after the lab crew came and went, but even so there wasn't much of a mess. But maybe the killer knew where to look. Did Crowe keep large sums of cash around the apartment?"

"I wouldn't know."

"Sure you would, but we'll let it pass. Maybe it was straight robbery and murder, with the killer forcing the old man to fork over the money, then killing him. Or maybe it was somebody with a reason to kill him, a motive. He have any enemies?"

"Not that I know of."

"Maybe he cheated somebody and yesterday it caught up with him. He had a long life. You can make a lot of enemies in seventy-one years."

"He was a nice man. He ate pastries and quoted Spinoza."

"And bought things from people who didn't own them."

I shrugged.

"Who did the Colcannon job?"

"How would I know?"

"You had some connection there, Bern. And one way or another Colcannon ties into Abel Crowe."

"How?"

"Maybe the old man set it up. Fences do that all the time, set up a place and get a burglar to knock it off. Maybe he did that and then there was an argument over the payoff. When Wanda Colcannon got killed maybe he decided there was more heat than he wanted to handle and he refused to buy whatever they stole, or wouldn't pay the price that was set in advance. Something like that."

"I suppose it's possible."

We batted it around until we were at the curb in front of Barnegat Books. I'd glanced at the Poodle Factory as we drove by and Carolyn was open for business. I started to thank Ray for the ride but he interrupted me with a heavy hand on my shoulder.

"You know more than you're lettin' on, Bern."

"I know it's hard enough to make a living selling used books. It's impossible if you never open the store."

"There's a killer out there," he said. "Maybe that's somethin' you oughta remember. He killed the Colcannon woman and he killed Crowe, and I'd say that's beginnin' to make him look like one dangerous son of a bitch."

"So?"

"So we'll pick him up before too long. Meanwhile, there's that Colcannon loot floatin' around, and who knows what else is up for grabs? And you always did have itchy fingers, Bern."

"I don't know what you're getting at."

" 'Course you don't. Just a couple of suggestions. If you know who did the killin', or if you happen to get wind of it, I'm the person you tell. Got that?"

"Fair enough."

"I'd like to bag whoever did it. Crowe was a nice old gentleman. The two times I met him, we never had anythin' we could make stick, nothin' that even came close, but he

was a gentleman all the same. What he was, he was generous." Free with a bribe, in other words. "And there's another
thing."

"Oh?"

"There's money in this, Bern. I keep gettin' this sense of
money, you know what I mean? I'd say I smell it, but that's
not it because it ain't a smell, it's a feel in the air. You know
what I mean?"

"I know what you mean."

"Like the feel right before it rains. So the thing is, Bern,
if you're out there and it starts rainin' money, don't forget
you got a partner."

Eleven

Carolyn came over around twelve-fifteen with a sack of carry-out from Mamoun's. We had a felafel sandwich apiece and split a side order of roasted peppers. They made a nice mint tea there and we each drank a container of it. The stuff comes with the sugar already in it, and that reminded Carolyn of the sugar hangover she'd had the day before, and that reminded her of Abel, and she wondered aloud what he was having for lunch, what sort of yummy good he was ingesting even as we spoke.

"He's not," I said.

"How do you know?"

"He's dead," I said, and while she sat staring at me I told her what I had learned from Ray Kirschmann. He had told me to remember I had a partner, and I had indeed remembered, but somehow I hadn't had the heart to go straight to the Poodle Factory and ruin Carolyn's day. So I'd opened the store instead, and dawdled in it, figuring it would be time enough when I saw her. Then she'd appeared with lunch and I had postponed the revelation so as to avoid ruining our appetites, and then, once the subject had come up, I'd blurted.

She listened all the way through, her frown deepening all the while. When I'd finished, and after we had spent a few minutes telling each other what a fine man Abel was and how obscene it was that he'd been murdered, she asked me who did it.

"No idea."

"You think it was the same ones who murdered Wanda Colcannon?"

"I don't see how. The police don't suspect a link between the Colcannon burglary and Abel's death. Ray does. He's positive there's a connection. But the only thing that connects Colcannon and Abel is us, and we're not connected with either one of the murders. So there's no real link between the house on West Eighteenth Street and the apartment on Riverside Drive, except that we took something from one place and left it at the other."

"Maybe that's the link."

"The coin?"

She nodded. "Twelve hours after we left it with him he was dead. Maybe someone killed him for it."

"Who?"

"I don't know."

"Who would even know he had it?"

"Somebody he was trying to sell it to."

I thought it over. "Maybe. Say he got up yesterday morning and called somebody to come over and have a look at the coin. Guy comes over, has a look, likes what he sees. More than that—one look and he knows he has to own the coin."

"But he can't afford it."

"Right. He can't afford it but he has to have it, and he gets carried away and picks up something heavy. Like what?"

"Who knows? A bookend, maybe."

A natural object for her to think of, given our surroundings. And, in those very surroundings, she had once picked up a bronze bust of Immanuel Kant which I'd been using as a bookend in the philosophy and religion section, only to bounce it off the skull of a murderer who'd been holding a gun on me at the time.

"Maybe a bookend," I agreed. "He gets carried away, brains Abel with the bookend, puts the 1913 V-Nickel in his pocket, and away he goes. And on his way he locks up after himself."

"Huh?"

"The doors were locked. Remember the police locks with the sliding bolts? The killer locked up after. Now I tend to do that after a burglary, picking the locks all over again, but who else do you know who does? And what passionate numismatist would think to do it, let alone have the ability?"

"Why wouldn't he just lock the door with Abel's keys?"

"Oh," I said.

"Did I say something wrong, Bern?"

"I would have thought of it myself sooner or later," I said sullenly. "In another minute I would have thought of it."

"It's just that you're not used to the idea of locking and unlocking doors with a key."

"Maybe."

"Anyway, it's interesting he thought of it. Most people would just get out of there and be satisfied with the lock that locks when you close the door."

"The spring lock."

"Right, the spring lock. But he must have wanted to keep the body from being discovered for as long as possible, and that mattered enough to him to make him take the trouble to find Abel's keys."

"Maybe he didn't have to look for them."

"Maybe. Even so—"

"Right," I said. "But so what? We still don't know anything much about him that we didn't know before we went through all this, except that he's reasonably clever and that he doesn't let a little thing like murder throw him off-stride.

I can't see any reason to suspect either set of Colcannon burglars. The ones that got there before we did were slobs. They would never know about Abel and they never would have been capable of getting into his apartment. They evidently stole a ton of stuff from the Colcannon house and they'll have to fence it somewhere or other, but I can't believe they tried to use Abel. Even if bunglers like that knew him, he'd be all wrong for what they stole. They must have loaded up on silver and furs, all the things Colcannon didn't keep in the safe, and Abel pretty much limited himself to stamps and coins and jewelry."

"And the ones who got there after we did?"

"The ones who killed Wanda Colcannon? We have to assume they just dropped in because the broken skylight looked like an engraved invitation. What quirk of fate do you figure got them all the way to Riverside Drive?"

"I guess they're out."

"I guess so. And I guess the cops'll have to work this one out for themselves, because I'm stumped. The best thing we've come up with so far is a homicidal numismatist who locks up after himself, and how many of those have you known in your life? I figure they're in the same category as hen's teeth and 1913 V-Nickels. I'm sorry he's dead, dammit. I liked him."

"So did I."

"And I'm sorry Wanda Colcannon's dead, even though I never met her. I'm sorry we got involved in this mess in the first place, and if I'm glad of anything it's that we're out of it. I think it's time I unlocked my own door again and tried selling a few books."

"I better get back myself. I got a dog to wash."

"Catch you later?"

"Sure."

Five hours later we were continuing our conversation at the Bum Rap, she with a martini, I with Scotch and water.

I'd had a long slow afternoon, the store full of customers who browsed endlessly without buying anything. On days like that it's murder trying to keep up with the shoplifters, and I'm pretty sure a studious lank-haired young woman got away with a copy of Sartre's *Being and Nothingness*. If she reads it, I figure that's punishment enough.

"I just hope the police wrap up both killers in a hurry," I told Carolyn. "We're out of it for the moment, and if they close both cases we'll stay out of it, and that would be fine with me."

"And if they don't?"

"Well, we *were* at Abel's place the night before last, and if they really dig they might try showing my picture to the doorman, and he might remember me. I told Ray I haven't been over there since July. There's no law against telling a lie to a policeman, but it doesn't make them look on you with favor. I've got an alibi, but I don't know how well it'll hold up."

"What alibi?"

"Denise."

"That's for last night, Bern. We were at Abel's the night before."

"Denise is my alibi for both nights."

"I hope she knows it."

"We talked about it."

"She knows about the Colcannon job?"

"She knows they suspected me. I told her I had nothing to do with the murder. I didn't mention that I happened to burgle the place earlier."

"Because she thinks you're retired."

"Something like that. At least she tells herself she thinks I'm retired. God knows what women think."

"So the bony blabbermouth is your alibi. I wondered why you were seeing her last night."

"That's not why."

"It's not?"

"It's not the only reason. I don't know what you've got against Denise. She always speaks well of you."

"The hell she does. She can't stand me."

"Well—"

"I don't know what kind of an alibi she'll make. She doesn't strike me as the type to lie convincingly. I hope you won't need her."

"So do I."

She signaled for another round of drinks. The waitress brought them to our table, and Carolyn's eyes followed her as she walked away. "She's new," she said. "What's her name, did you happen to notice?"

"I think someone called her Angela."

"Pretty name."

"I suppose."

"She's pretty, too. Don't you think?"

"She's all right."

"Probably straight." She drank some of her martini. "What do you think?"

"About the waitress?"

"Yeah. Angela."

"What about her? Whether she's straight or gay?"

"Yeah."

"How should I know?"

"Well, you could have an impression."

"I don't," I said. "All I've noticed is what she plays on the jukebox. Fall in love with her and you'll spend the rest of your life listening to country and western. You'll have Barbara Mandrell coming out of your ears. Could we forget about Angela for a minute?"

"You could. I'm not sure I can. Yeah, sure, Bern. What is it?"

"Well, I was thinking about Abel. About the murderous coin collector who did him in."

"And?"

"And I don't believe it," I said. "The timing's no good. Say he goes to sleep right after we leave, gets up first thing in the morning and calls a collector. The guy comes over almost immediately, kills Abel and leaves. That's about how it would have had to happen, and Abel wouldn't work it that way. He'd have wanted to turn it over quickly, but not that quickly. First he'd want to convince himself the coin was genuine, and didn't he say something about X-raying it? He'd have done that first, and he'd have waited to see what kind of heat the Colcannon job generated, and if the theft of the V-Nickel was reported in the press. That would help determine the price he could charge for it, so he wouldn't sell it until he had the information. I don't think his murder had a damned thing to do with that coin, because I don't think anyone in the world outside of you and me had the slightest idea that he had it. Nobody followed us there. Nobody saw us walk in. And we didn't tell anybody anything. At least I didn't."

"Who would I tell? You're the only person who knows I ever do anything besides groom dogs."

"Then someone had another reason for killing Abel. Maybe it was a straight and simple robbery. Maybe somebody else tried to sell him something and they argued. Or maybe it was someone from his past."

"You mean Dachau? Someone he knew in the concentration camp?"

"It's possible, or maybe someone from his more recent past. I don't know much about him. I know Crowe's not the name he was born with. He told me once that his name was originally Amsel, which means blackbird in German. From blackbird to crow is a simple leap. But another time he told me the same story except the name wasn't Amsel, it was Schwarzvogel. That means blackbird, too, but you'd think he'd remember which one of the words was his original name. Unless neither was."

"He was Jewish, wasn't he?"

"I don't think so."

"Then what was he doing in Dachau?"

"You know the rye-bread ads? 'You don't have to be Jewish to love Levy's.' Well, you didn't have to be Jewish to go to Dachau. Abel told me he was a political prisoner, a Social Democrat. That may have been the truth, or he could have landed there for some ordinary crime—receiving stolen goods, for instance. Or maybe he was gay. That was another good way to get to Dachau."

She shuddered.

"The thing is," I went on, "I don't know a hell of a lot about Abel's past. It's possible nobody does. But he could have made an enemy along the way. Or it could have been a robbery or a disagreement or any damned thing. If he *was* gay, for example, maybe he brought a hustler home and got killed out of simple meanness, or for the money in his wallet."

"It happens all the time. Do you really think he could have been gay, Bern? He kept trying to marry the two of us off. If he was gay himself, wouldn't he have been quicker to pick up on the fact that I'm not your standard marriage material?" She finished her drink. "And isn't the whole thing too much of a coincidence? His death and Wanda's death, one right after the other?"

"Only because we're the link between them. But we're not connected with their deaths, and we're the only link between them otherwise, you and I and the nickel. And that's no link at all."

"I guess not."

I made interlocking rings on the tabletop with the wet bottom of my Scotch glass. "Maybe I'm just telling myself this because it's what I want to believe," I said. "Except that I'm not altogether sure I want to believe it anyway, because of where it leads."

"You just lost me."

"The nickel," I said. "The 1913 V-Nickel, the Colcannon nickel, the one we could have taken $17,500 for if we hadn't picked pie in the sky instead."

"Don't remind me."

"If he wasn't killed for the nickel," I said, "and if he was murdered by some clown who didn't even *know* about the nickel, don't you see what that means?"

"Oh."

"Right. The nickel's still there."

I spent the evening at home. Dinner was a can of chili with some extra cumin and cayenne stirred in to pep it up. I ate it in front of the television set and kept it company with a bottle of Carta Blanca. I caught the tail end of the local news while the chili was heating. There was a brief and uninformative item about Abel, nothing about the Colcannon burglary. I watched John Chancellor while I ate, and I sat through half of *Family Feud* before I overcame inertia sufficiently to get up and turn it off.

I tidied up, stacked a mix of jazz and classical music on the record player, settled in with the latest *Antiquarian Bookman,* a magazine consisting almost exclusively of dealers' lists of books they wish to acquire for resale. I scanned the ads lazily, making a mark now and then when I found something I remembered having in stock. Several of the marks I made were for books presently reposing on my bargain table, and if I could sell them to someone who was actively seeking them I could certainly get more than forty cents apiece for them.

If I took the trouble to write to the advertisers and wait for their orders and wrap the books and ship them. That was the trouble with the used-book business. There were so many niggling things you had to attend to, so much watching the pence in hope that the pounds would take care of themselves. I didn't make a decent living from Barnegat Books, didn't even make a profit at it, but I probably could have if I'd had that infinite capacity for taking pains that success seems to demand.

The thing is, I love the book business. But I like to do it my way, which is to say in a distinctly casual fashion. Burglary spoils one. When you've grown accustomed to turning a big dollar in a few hours by means of illegal entry, it's hard to work up much enthusiasm for a lot of routine work that won't yield more than the price of a movie ticket.

Still, it was fun reading through the ads and checking off titles. Even if I'd probably never follow it up.

I called Denise around nine. Jared answered, told me *Babel-17* was all he'd hoped it would be, then summoned his mother to the phone. We talked for a few minutes about nothing in particular. Carolyn's name came up, I don't remember how, and Denise referred to her as "that lesbian dwarf, the fat little one who always smells of Wet Dog."

"Funny," I said, "she always speaks well of you."

Carolyn called a little later. "I was thinking about what we were talking about," she said. "You're not going to do anything about it, are you?"

"I guess not."

"Because it's impossible, Bern. Remember the conversation we had with Abel? The fire escape's on the front of the building and he's got gates on the window anyway. And the doorman takes his job twice as seriously as Saint Peter, and there are those police locks on the doors—"

"There used to be," I said, "but the cops got a locksmith to open one of them."

"What's the difference? You still can't get into the building."

"I know."

"And it's driving you crazy, isn't it?"

"How'd you guess?"

"Because it's driving me crazy, too. Bernie, if we hadn't already stolen the damned coin once, and all you knew about it was that it was probably somewhere in that apartment, an apartment the police have probably sealed off because someone was killed in it yesterday, and you knew what kind of security they have in the building and all, and you knew that the coin was probably hidden somewhere in the apartment and that you wouldn't even know where to start looking for it, assuming it was there in the first place, which you can't be positive of—"

"I get the picture, Carolyn."

"Well, assuming all that, would you even think twice about stealing the coin?"

"Of course not."

"That's what I mean."

"But we already stole it once."

"I know."

"And that makes me tend to think of it as my coin," I explained. "They say thieves don't respect private property. Well, I have a very strongly developed sense of private property, as long as it's my property we're talking about. And it's not just the money, either. I had a great rarity in my hands and now I've got nothing. Think what a blow that is to the old self-esteem."

"So what are you going to do about it?"

"Nothing."

"That's good."

"Because there's nothing I *can* do."

"Right. That's what I wanted to check, Bern. I'm on my way over to the Duchess. Maybe I'll get lucky and meet somebody sensational."

"Good luck."

"I'm so goddamn restless lately. Must be a full moon. Maybe I'll run into Angela. She'll be feeding the jukebox and playing all the Anne Murray records. I guess she must be straight, huh?"

"Anne Murray?"

"Angela. Figure she's straight?"

"Probably."

"If she's straight and Abel was gay they could have raised poodles together."

"And you could have clipped them."

"I could have clipped the poodles, too. Jesus, how do I get out of this conversation?"

"I don't know. Which way did you get in?"

"Bye, Bern."

The eleven o'clock news brought no fresh revelations, and who wants a stale one? I turned the set off as soon as they'd announced who Johnny's guests were, grabbed a jacket and went out. I hiked up West End Avenue, took a left at Eighty-sixth, walked the rest of the way on Riverside Drive.

The air was cooler now, and heavy with impending rain. You couldn't see any stars but you hardly ever can in New York, even on cloudless nights. The pollution's always thick enough to obscure them. I did see a moon, about half full with a haze around it. That means something, either that it's going to rain or it isn't, but I can never remember which.

There were a surprising number of people on the street— joggers plodding around Riverside Park, dog owners walking their pets, other people bringing home a quart of milk and the early edition of the *Times*. I crossed the street for a better view and looked up at Abel's building, counting floors to find his window. It was dark, naturally enough. I let my eyes travel around the corner and noted the fire escape on the Eighty-ninth Street side. It looked substantial enough, but it was right out there in plain view and you couldn't reach the bottom rungs from the sidewalk unless you had a long ladder.

Pointless anyway. As Carolyn had made quite clear.

I walked toward Ninetieth Street. The building immediately adjacent to Abel's stood three stories taller, which meant I couldn't get from its roof to Abel's unless I was prepared to lower myself on a rope. I wasn't, nor did I have any reason to assume security there would be any less rigid than at its neighbor. I returned to Eighty-ninth Street and walked a few doors past Abel's building. It was bounded on that side by a long row of late-nineteenth-century brownstones, all of them four stories tall. The windows in Abel's building that looked out over the brownstones were too high to be readily accessible from the rooftop, and there were steel guards over them anyway.

I started walking toward West End Avenue again, then doubled back for another look, feeling like an addled criminal drawn irresistibly back to the scene of someone else's crime. The doorman was the same stiff-spined black man who'd been on duty during our previous visit, and he looked as formidable as ever. I watched him from across the street. Waste of time, I told myself. I wasn't accomplishing anything. I was as restless as Carolyn and instead of going to the Duchess I was going through the motions.

I crossed the street, approached the entrance. The building was a massive old pile of brick, safe as a fortress and solid as the Bank of England. Engaged columns of a dull red marble flanked the double entrance doors. Bronze plaques on either side announced the professional tenants within. I noted three shrinks, a dentist, an ophthalmologist, a podiatrist and a pediatrician, a fairly representative Upper West Side mix.

I saw no plaque for Abel Crowe, Receiver of Stolen Goods, and I shook my head at the thought. Give me half a chance and I can become disgustingly maudlin.

The doorman approached, asked if he could help me. I got the feeling he'd lately graduated with honors from an assertiveness-training workshop.

"No," I said sadly. "Too late for that." And I turned away and went home.

The phone rang while I unlocked all of my locks and gave up in mid-ring as I was shoving the door open. If it's important, I told myself, they'll call back.

I took a shower which no one could have called prema-
ture, got into bed, dozed off. I was dreaming about a perilous
descent—a fire escape, a catwalk, something vague—when
the phone rang. I sat up, blinked a few times, answered it.

"I want the coin," a male voice said.

"Huh?"

"The nickel. I want it."

"Who is this?"

"Not important. You have the coin and I want it. Don't
dispose of it. I'll contact you."

"But—"

The phone clicked in my ear. I fumbled it back onto the
receiver. The bedside clock said it was a quarter to two. I
hadn't been sleeping long, just long enough to get into the
swing of it. I lay down and reviewed the phone call and tried
to decide whether to get up and do something about it.

While I was thinking it over I fell back asleep.

Twelve

Murray Feinsinger's goatee had just a touch of gray in it a little to the right of center. He looked to be around forty, with a round face, a receding hairline, and massive horn-rimmed glasses that had the effect of magnifying his brown eyes. He was kneeling now and looking up at me, with my shoe in one hand and my bare foot in the other. My sock lay on the floor beside him like a dead laboratory rat.

"Narrow feet," he said. "Long, narrow feet."

"Is that bad?"

"Only if it's extreme, and yours aren't. Just a little narrower than average, but you're wearing Pumas, which are a little wider than average. Not as much so as the wide versions of shoes that come in widths, but what do you need with extra width when you've got a narrow foot to begin with? Your feet wind up with too much room and that increases the tendency of the ankle to pronate. That means it turns in, like this"—he positioned my foot for demonstration—"and that's the source of all your problems."

"I see."

"New Balance makes variable widths. You could try a pair

on for size. Or there's Brooks—they make a good shoe and they're a little on the narrow side, and they ought to fit you fine."

"That's great," I said, and would have gotten up from the chair, except it's tricky when somebody's holding one of your feet. "I'll just get a new pair of shoes," I said, "and then I'll be all set."

"Not so fast, my friend. How long have you been running?"

"Not very long."

"Matter of fact, you just started. Am I right?"

As a matter of fact, I hadn't even started, and didn't intend to. But I told him he was right. And then I emitted a foolish little giggle, not because anything struck me funny but because the good Dr. Feinsinger was tickling my foot.

"That tickle?"

"A little."

"Inhibition," he said. "That's what makes tickling. I tickle people day in and day out. No avoiding it when you've got your hands full of other people's feet for six or eight hours at a stretch. Ever tickle your own feet?"

"I never gave it a thought."

"Well, trust me—you couldn't do it if you tried. It wouldn't work. The ticklishness is a response to being touched in a certain way by another person. Inhibition. That's what it's all about."

"That's very interesting," I said. Untruthfully.

"I tickle a patient less over a period of time. Not that I touch him differently. But he gets used to my touch. Less inhibited. That's what tickling's all about. And what your feet are all about, my friend, is something else again. Know what you've got?"

Five toes on each of them, I thought, and a loquacious podiatrist for company. But evidently it was something more serious than that. I hadn't expected this.

"You've got Morton's Foot," he said.

"I do?"

"No question about it." He curled his index finger and flicked it sharply against my index toe. "Morton's Foot. Know what that means?"

Death, I thought. Or amputation, or thirty years in a wheelchair, and at the least I'd never play the piano again. "I really don't know," I admitted. "I suppose it has something to do with salt."

"Salt?" He looked confused, but only for a moment. "Morton's Foot," he said, and flicked my toe again. It didn't tickle, so maybe I was overcoming my inhibitions. "Sounds ominous, doesn't it? All it means is that this toe here"— another flick—"is longer than your big toe. Morton's the doctor who first described the syndrome, and what it amounts to is a structural weakness of the foot. I have a hunch it's a throwback to the time when we all lived in trees and used our big toes as thumbs and wrapped our second toes around vines and branches for leverage. Next time you get to the Bronx Zoo, make sure you go to the monkey house and look at the little buggers' feet."

"I'll do that."

"Not that Morton's Foot is like being born with a tail, for God's sake. In fact, it's more common to have Morton's Foot than not to have it, which is bad news for runners but good news for podiatrists. So you've not only got a nasty-sounding complaint, my friend, but you've got a very *ordinary* nasty-sounding complaint."

All my life the only trouble I'd had with my feet was when some klutz stepped on them on the subway. Of course I'd never tried wrapping my toes around vines. I asked Feinsinger if what I had was serious.

"Not if you live a normal life. But runners"—and he chuckled with real pleasure here—"runners give up normal life the day they buy their first pair of waffle trainers. That's when Morton's Foot starts causing problems. Pain in the ball of the foot, for example. Heel spurs, for instance. Shin splints. Achilles tendinitis. Excessive pronation—remember our old friend pronation?" And he refreshed my memory by yanking my ankle inward. "And then," he said darkly, "there's always chondromalacia."

"There is?"

He nodded with grim satisfaction. "Chondromalacia. The dreaded Runner's Knee, every bit as fearful as Tennis Elbow."

"It sounds terrible."

"Potentially terrible. But never fear," he added brightly, "for Feinsinger's here, and relief is right around the corner. All you need is the right pair of custom orthotics and you can run until your heart gives out. And for that I'll refer you to my brother-in-law Ralph. He's the cardiologist in the family." He patted my foot. "Just my little joke. Stay with running and the chances are you won't *need* a cardiologist. It's the best thing you can do for yourself. All we have to do is make sure your feet are up to it, and that's where I come in."

Orthotics, it turned out, were little inserts for me to wear in my shoes. They would be custom-made for me out of layers of leather and cork after the good Dr. Feinsinger took impressions of my feet, which he did right there and then before I had much of a chance to think about what I was getting into. He took my bare feet one at a time and pressed them into a box containing something like styrofoam, except softer.

"You've made a good first impression," he assured me. "Now come into the other room for a moment, my friend. I want to have a look at your bones."

I followed him, walking springily on the balls of my feet, while he told me how my personal pair of orthotics would not only enable me to run without pain but were virtually certain to change my whole life, improve my posture and penmanship, and very likely elevate my character in the bargain. He led me into a cubicle down the hall where a menacing contraption with a faintly dental air about it was mounted on the wall. He had me sit in a chair and swung the gadget out from the wall so that a cone-shaped protuberance was centered over my right foot.

"I don't know about this," I said.

"Guaranteed painless. Trust me, friend."

"You hear a lot of things about X-rays, don't you? Sterility, things like that."

"All I take is a one-second exposure and nothing goes higher than the ankle. Sterility? There's such a thing as the ball of the foot, my friend, but unless you've actually got your balls in your feet I assure you you've got nothing to worry about."

In a matter of minutes the machine had done its nasty work and I was back in the other room pulling up my socks and lacing up my Pumas. They had never felt wide before, but they certainly felt wide now. With every step I took I imagined my Mortonic feet slipping dangerously from side to side. Heel spurs, shin splints, the dreaded Runner's Knee—

And then we were back in the reception room where I let a redhead with a Bronx accent book an appointment three weeks hence for me to pick up my orthotics. "The full price is three hundred dollars," she told me, "and that includes the lab charges and this visit and all subsequent visits, in case you need any adjustments. It's a one-time charge and there's nothing additional, and of course it's fully deductible for taxes."

"Three hundred dollars," I said.

"No cost compared to other sports," Feinsinger said. "Look what you'd spend on a single ski weekend, let alone buying your equipment. Look at the hourly rates they're getting for tennis courts. All you have to do to get the full benefits of running is get out there and run, and isn't it worth it to spend a few dollars on the only feet God gave you?"

"And running's good for me, I guess."

"Best thing in the world for you. Improves your cardiovascular system, tones your muscles, keeps you trim and fit. But your feet take a pounding, and if they're not set up to handle the task—"

Three hundred dollars still seemed pretty pricey for a custom version of the little arch supports they sell for $1.59 at the corner drugstore. But it dawned on me that I didn't have to pay it now, that a thirty-dollar deposit would keep everybody happy, and in three weeks' time they could sit around wondering why I hadn't shown up. I handed over three tens and pocketed the receipt the redhead handed me.

"Running must be great for podiatrists," I ventured.

Feinsinger beamed. "Nothing like it," he said. "Nothing in the world. You know what this business was a few years ago? Old ladies with feet that hurt. Of course they hurt, they weighed three hundred pounds and bought shoes that were too small. I removed corns, I wrapped bunions, I did a little of this and a little of that and I told myself I was a professional person and success wasn't all that important to me.

"Now it's a whole new world. Sports podiatry is my entire practice. Feinsinger orthotics were on the road in Boston last month. Feinsinger orthotics carried dozens upon dozens of runners to the finish line of the New York Marathon last October. I have patients who love me. They know I'm helping them and they love me. And I'm a success. You're lucky I had a cancellation this morning or I'd never have been able to fit you in. I'm booked way in advance. And you want to know something? I like success. I like getting ahead in the world. You get a taste of it, my friend, and you develop an appetite for it."

He dropped an arm around my shoulders, led me through a waiting room where several slender gentlemen sat reading back copies of *Runner's World* and *Running Times*. "I'll see you in three weeks," he said. "Meanwhile you can run in the shoes you're wearing. Don't buy new shoes because you'll want to have the orthotics when you try 'em on. Just go nice and easy for the time being. Not too far and not too fast, and I'll see you in three weeks."

Out in the hallway, the Pumas felt incredibly clumsy. Odd I'd never noticed their ungainly width in the past. I walked on down the carpeted hall to the elevator, glanced over my shoulder, looked around furtively, and went on past the elevator to open the door to the stairwell.

I wasn't sure what effect Morton's Foot might have on stairclimbing. Was I running a heavy risk of the dreaded Climber's Fetlock?

I went ahead and took my chances. Murray Feinsinger's office was on the fourth floor, which left me with seven flights to ascend. I was panting long before I reached my destination, either because my feet lacked the benefit of orthotics or because my cardiovascular system had not yet been improved by long-distance running. Or both of the above.

Whatever the cause, a minute or two was time enough for me to catch my breath. Then I eased the door open, looked both ways much like a tractable child about to cross a street, and walked past the elevator and down another carpeted hallway to the door of Abel Crowe's apartment.

Well, why else would I be getting my feet tickled? I had awakened a few hours earlier, had a shower and a shave, and while I sat spreading gooseberry preserves on an English muffin and waiting for my coffee to drip through, I recalled my reconnaissance mission to Riverside Drive and the telephone call that had interrupted my sleep.

Someone wanted the coin.

That wasn't news. When an object originally valued at five cents has increased over the years by a factor of approximately ten million, the world is full of people who wouldn't be averse to calling it their own. Who wouldn't want a 1913 Liberty Head Nickel?

But my caller not only wanted the coin. He wanted it from me. Which meant he knew the coin had been liberated from

Colcannon's safe, and he knew furthermore just who had been the instrument of its delivery.

Who was he? And how might he know a little thing or two like that?

I poured my coffee, munched my muffin, and sat a while in uffish thought. I found myself thinking of that impregnable fortress where my friend Abel had lived and died, and where the coin—my coin!—survived him. I pictured that doorman, a gold-braided Cerberus at the gate of hell, a three-headed Bouvier des Flandres in burgundy livery. (The old mind's not at its best first thing in the morning, but the imagination is capable of great flights of fancy.) I visualized that entrance, those dull rosy marble columns, the bronze plaques. Three shrinks, a dentist, a pediatrician, a podiatrist, an ophthalmologist—

Whereupon dawn broke.

I finished breakfast and became very busy. I hadn't remembered the names on those plaques, or bothered noticing them in the first place, so for openers I cabbed up to Eighty-ninth and Riverside, where I sauntered nonchalantly past the entrance and quickly memorized the seven names in question. A few doors down the street I took a moment to jot them all down before they fled my memory, and then I continued east to Broadway where I had a cup of coffee at the counter of a Cuban Chinese luncheonette. Perhaps the Cuban food's good there, or the Chinese food. The coffee tasted as though each roasted bean had been tossed lightly in rancid butter before grinding.

I turned a dollar into dimes and made phone calls. I tried the psychiatrists first and found them all booked up through the following week. I made an appointment with the last of them for a week from Monday, figuring I could always show up for it if nothing else materialized by then, by which time a shrink's services might be just what I needed.

Then I looked at the four remaining names. The pediatrician would be tricky, I decided, unless I wanted to borrow

Jared Raphaelson for the occasion, and I wasn't sure that I did. The dentist might be able to fit me in, especially if I pleaded an emergency, but did I want some unknown quantity belaboring my mouth? As things stand, I get free lifetime dental care from Craig Sheldrake, the World's Greatest Dentist, and I'd last seen Craig just a couple of weeks ago when I'd dropped by for a cleaning. My mouth was in no need of a dentist's attention, and I didn't feel much like saying Ah.

The ophthalmologist looked like the best choice, better even than the shrinks. An eye exam doesn't take long, either. I'd have to make sure he didn't put drops in my eyes, since that could make lockpicking a far cry from child's play. And wasn't I about due to get my eyes looked at? I had never needed glasses, and I hadn't yet noticed myself holding books at arm's length, but neither was I getting younger with each passing day, and they say it's a good idea to get your eyes checked annually so that you can nip glaucoma in the bud, or the pupil or iris, or wherever one nips it, and—

And I made the call and the guy was in the Bahamas until a week from Monday.

So I called Murray Feinsinger's office, wondering upon what pretext a podiatric appointment might be booked, and a young woman with a Bronx accent (and, I was to learn, with red hair as well) asked me the nature of my problem.

"It's my feet," I said.

"You a runner or a dancer?"

Dancers look like dancers. Anybody can look like a runner. All you have to do is sweat and wear funny shoes.

"A runner," I said, and she gave me an appointment.

Whereupon I went home and changed my Weejuns for my Pumas, all in the interest of verisimilitude, and then I called Carolyn and begged out of our standing lunch date, pleading a doctor's appointment. She wanted to know what kind of doctor, and I said an ophthalmologist instead of a podiatrist because I'd have been stuck for an answer if she asked what was the matter with my feet. I didn't yet know I had Morton's foot, with chondromalacia just a hop, skip and a jump away. When she asked what was the matter with my eyes, I muttered something about getting headaches when I did a lot of reading, and that seemed to satisfy her.

I didn't mention the middle-of-the-night phone call.

At one-fifteen I showed for my appointment with Feinsinger. The doorman called upstairs to make sure I was expected and the elevator operator lingered to check that I entered the right door. Now I was out thirty bucks and my feet felt too narrow while my shoes felt impossibly wide. Maybe I should have gone to the pediatrician instead. I could have lied about my age.

I put my ear to Abel's door, listened carefully, heard nothing. There was a button recessed in the doorjamb and I gave it a poke, and a muted bong sounded within the apartment. I heard no other sound in response to the bong, nor did a brisk knock provoke any reaction, so I took a deep breath, drew the tools of my trade from my pocket, and opened the door.

It was at least as easy as it sounds. The police had slapped a sticker on the door forbidding entry to anyone other than authorized police personnel, which I emphatically was not, but they hadn't taken the trouble to seal the apartment in any meaningful fashion, perhaps because the building's security was so forbidding. The locksmith who'd knocked off Abel's police lock (by drilling the cylinder rather than picking it, I noted with some professional disapproval) had left only the door's original lock as a deterrent to entry. It was a Segal, with both an automatic spring lock that engaged when you closed the door and a deadbolt that you had to turn with a key. The cops had probably had keys—they could have obtained one from the doorman or the super—but the last man out hadn't bothered to use one, because only the spring lock secured the door, and it was no harder to open than those childproof bottles of aspirin. It would have been faster if I'd had the key, but just barely.

I stepped inside, drew the door shut, turned the little knob to engage the deadbolt. I hesitated in the foyer, trying to figure out what was wrong. Something was bothering me and I couldn't pin it down.

The hell with it. I moved from the dimness of the foyer into the living room, where light streamed in through the windows. Near the window on the left I saw an outline in chalk, half on the burnished parquet floor and half on the oriental rug. The rug was a Sarouk and it was a nice one and the chalk marks didn't do anything for it.

Looking at the outline, I could picture his body lying there, one arm outstretched, one leg pointing directly at the chair where I'd been sitting Tuesday night. I didn't want to look at the chalk marks and I didn't seem able to keep my eyes away from them. I felt funny. I turned away from them and turned back again, and then I skirted the chalk marks and walked to the window and looked out over the park, out across the river.

And then I realized what had been bothering me in the foyer. It was an absence that I had been faintly aware of, as Sherlock Holmes had remarked on the dog's not barking in the night.

The thrill was gone. That little boost I always get when I cross a threshold without an invitation, that little up feeling that comes on like coffee in a vein, simply wasn't there. I had come as a burglar, had managed entry by means of my cleverness and my skills, yet I felt neither triumph nor anticipation.

Because it was my old friend's place and he had lately died in it, and that took the joy out of the occupation.

I gazed at New Jersey in the distance—which is where it belongs. The sky had darkened in the few minutes since I'd entered the apartment. It looked like rain, which would

112

mean either that the haze around last night's moon had been an accurate forecaster or that it had not, depending on what it's supposed to herald.

I felt a little better once I knew what was bothering me. Now I could forget about it and get on with the business of robbing the dead.

Of course that's not what I was doing. I was merely bent on recovering what was rightfully mine—or wrongfully mine, if you want to be technical about it. By no stretch of the imagination could the coin be considered Abel's property; he'd had it strictly on consignment, having neither bought nor stolen it from me.

So all I had to do was find it.

I suppose I could have aped the method of the clods who'd preceded us to the Colcannon house. The fastest way to search a place is to let the chips fall where they may, along with everything else. But that would have made it quite obvious that someone had come a-hunting, and what was the point of that? And, even if I hadn't cared about that, I'm neat by inclination, and particularly indisposed to desecrate the home of a departed friend.

Abel too had been neat. There was a place for everything and everything was already in it, and I took care to put it all back where I'd found it.

This made the process difficult beyond description. The proverbial needle in the proverbial haystack would have been a piece of cake in comparison. I started off looking in the obvious places because that's where people hide things, even the people you'd think would know better. But I found nothing but water and Ty-D-bol in his toilet tank and nothing but flour in the flour canister and nothing but air in the hollow towel bars I unbolted from the bathroom wall. I pulled out drawers to see what was taped to their backs or bottoms. I went through the closets and checked suit pockets, thrust my hands inside shoes and boots, looked under rugs.

I could go step by step and fill a dozen pages with an explanation of the search I gave those rooms, but what's the point? Three things I didn't find were the philosopher's stone, the Holy Grail, and the golden fleece. A fourth was the Colcannon V-Nickel.

I did find any number of other interesting articles. I found books in several languages ranging in value to over a thousand dollars. It was no great accomplishment finding them; they constituted Abel Crowe's personal library and were out in the open on his shelves.

I looked behind each book, and I flipped the pages of each book, and I found nineteenth-century postage stamps from Malta and Cyprus in the pages of Hobbes's *Leviathan* and five hundred pounds in British currency tucked into a copy of *Sartor Resartus,* by Thomas Carlyle. On a high shelf I found what were probably Sassanian coins tucked behind three leatherbound volumes of the poetry of Byron and Shelley and Keats.

There were two telephones in the bedroom, one on the bedside table, the other across the room on a dresser. That seemed excessive. I checked, and both of them were hooked up to wall plugs, but the one on the dresser didn't seem to be in working order. So I unscrewed the base plate and discovered that the thing had been gutted, its working parts replaced with a wad of fifties and hundreds. I counted up to $20,000, which brought me close enough to the end of the stack to estimate that it totaled perhaps $23,000 in all. I put the phone back together again, with the money back inside where I'd found it.

That's enough to give you the idea. I found no end of valuable booty, which is just what you'd expect to find in the home of a civilized and prosperous fence. I found more cash, more stamps, more coins, and a fair amount of jewelry, including the watch and earrings from the Colcannon burglary. (They were in a humidor beneath a layer of cigars. I got excited when I came upon them, thinking the nickel might be nearby, but it wasn't. I'd never known Abel to smoke a cigar.)

In his kitchen, I helped myself to a piece of dense chocolatey layer cake. I think it was of the sort he called Schwarzwälder kuchen. Black Forest cake. Except for that and the glass of milk I drank along with it, I took nothing whatsoever from Abel Crowe's apartment.

I thought of it. Every time I hit something really tempting I tried to talk myself into it, and I just couldn't manage it. You'd think it would have been easy to rationalize. As far as I knew, Abel had no heirs. If an heir did turn up, he'd probably never see half the swag stashed in that apartment. The library would be sold *en bloc* to a book dealer, who in turn would profit handsomely enough reselling the volumes individually without ever discovering the bonuses that some of them contained. The watch and earrings would wind up the property of the first cigar smoker to wander in, while the $23,000 would stay in the telephone forever. What happens to telephones when somebody dies? Do they go back to the phone company? If they don't work, does somebody repair them? Whoever repaired this particular one was in for the surprise of his life.

So why didn't I help myself?

I guess I just plain found out that robbing the dead was not something I was prepared to do. Not the newly dead, anyway. Not a dead friend. All things considered, I'll be damned if I can think of a single logical argument against robbing the dead. One would think they'd mind it a good deal less than the living. If they can't take it with them, why should they care where it goes?

And God knows the dead do get robbed. Cops do it all the time. When a derelict dies in a Bowery flophouse, the first thing the officers on the scene do is divvy up whatever cash they find. Admittedly I've always set higher standards for myself than those of a policeman, but my standards weren't all that lofty, were they?

It was hard leaving the cash. When I've broken into a home or place of business I invariably take whatever cash presents itself. Even if I've entered the place for some other purpose, I still pocket cash automatically, reflexively. I don't have to think about it. I just do it.

This time I didn't. Oddly enough, I came close to taking the Piaget watch and the emerald earrings. Not that I found them tempting, but because I thought I might take them with something approaching legitimacy. After all, Carolyn and I had stolen them to begin with.

But we had been paid for them, hadn't we? So they weren't ours any longer. They were Abel's, and they would remain in his apartment.

One of the books I paged through was the copy of Spinoza's *Ethics* we'd brought him, and when I'd run out of places to search I took it down from its shelf and flipped idly through it. Abel had made shelf space for it on the last night of his life. Perhaps he'd paused first to thumb through it, reading a sentence here, a paragraph there.

"It may easily come to pass," I read, *"that a vain man may become proud and imagine himself pleasing to all when he is in reality a universal nuisance."*

I took the book with me when I left. I don't know why. It was Abel's property—a gift is a gift, after all—but I somehow felt entitled to reclaim it.

I guess I just hate to leave a place empty-handed.

Thirteen

I would have taken the stairs as far as Murray Feinsinger's floor, on the chance that the same elevator operator was on the job and that his memory was working overtime. But as I neared the elevator an elderly woman slowed me with a nod and a smile. She was wearing a black Persian lamb jacket and held a very small dog in her arms. It might have been a Maltese. Carolyn would have known at a glance.

"You'll be caught in the rain," she told me. "Go back and get your raincoat."

"I'm running late as it is."

"I have a plastic raincoat," she said. "Folded, and in my purse at all times." She patted her shoulder bag. "You're the Stettiner boy, aren't you? How's your mother?"

"Oh, she's fine."

"The sore throat's better?"

"Much better."

"That's good to hear," she said, and scratched the little dog behind the ear. "It must be doing her a world of good to have you home for a few days. You'll be here how long? The weekend or a little longer?"

"Well, as long as I can."

"Wonderful," she said. The elevator arrived, the door opened. I followed her onto it. The same operator was indeed running the car, but there was no recognition in his eyes. "You wouldn't remember me," the woman said. "I'm Mrs. Pomerance in 11-J."

"Of course I remember you, Mrs. Pomerance."

"And your mother's feeling better? I'm trying to remember the last time I talked with her. I was so sorry to hear about her brother. Your uncle."

What about him? "Well," I said, tightening my grip on Spinoza, "these things happen."

"His heart, wasn't it?"

"That's right."

"Listen, it's not the worst way. You must have heard about our neighbor? Mr. Crowe in 11-D?"

"Yes, I heard. Just the other day, wasn't it?"

"The day before yesterday, they say. You've heard what they're saying about him? That he bought from thieves? It was in the papers. Imagine in this building, after the co-op conversion and everything, and one of the residents is a man who buys from thieves. And then to be struck down and killed in his own apartment."

"Terrible."

We had reached the ground floor and walked together through the lobby. Just inside the entrance she stopped to clip a leash to the little dog's collar, then extracted a folded plastic raincoat from her bag. "I'll just carry this over my arm," she said, "so that when it starts raining I won't have to go looking for it. That Mr. Crowe—it makes a person think. He was always a nice man, he always had time for a kind word on the elevator. If he was a criminal, you would still have to say he was a good neighbor."

We strolled past the doorman, hesitated beneath the canopy. The little dog was pulling at his leash, anxious to head west toward Riverside Park. I was at least as anxious to head east.

"Well," I said, "he was a fence."

"That's the word. A fence."

"And you know what they say. Good fences make good neighbors."

There was no point going downtown. It was already past closing time when I left Abel's apartment. I got a bus on Broadway, not wanting to get caught in the rain with Spinoza under my arm. The rain was still holding off when I got off at Seventy-second Street and walked home.

Nothing but bills and circulars in my mailbox. I carried them upstairs, threw away the offers from those who wanted to sell me something, filed the demands from those who wished to be paid. Getting and spending we lay waste our powers, I thought, and put Spinoza up there on the shelf alongside of Wordsworth.

I called Carolyn's apartment. She didn't answer. I called Narrowback Gallery and Jared answered and told me his mother was out. I called the Poodle Factory and got Carolyn's machine. I didn't leave a message.

I hung up the phone and it rang before I could get three steps away from it. I picked it up and said hello. I was about to say hello a second time when it clicked in my ear.

A wrong number. Or my caller of the night before. Or some friend who'd decided at the last moment that she didn't really want to talk to me tonight after all. Or someone, anyone, who'd merely wanted to establish that I was at home.

Or none of the above.

I got an umbrella, started for the door. The phone rang again. I let myself out, locked up after me. The ringing followed me down the hall.

*   *   *

A block away on Broadway I had a big plate of spaghetti and a large green salad with oil and vinegar. I hadn't had anything since breakfast aside from the cake and milk at Abel's apartment, and I was hungry and angry and lonely and tired, and the first of the four seemed the only one I could do anything about for the moment. Afterward I had a small portion of tortoni, which never turns out to be as interesting a dessert as one would hope, and with it I drank four tiny cups of inky espresso in quick succession, each flavored with just a drop of anisette. By the time I got out of there caffeine was perking through my veins. I was neither hungry nor tired now, and it was hard to remember what I'd been angry about. I was still lonely but I figured I could live with it.

I walked home through the rain, and I couldn't see the moon to check whether it had a haze around it. When I got back to my building, the usually stolid Armand greeted me by name. He had managed to ignore me when I'd come in earlier, and when I'd left for the restaurant. He and Felix are quite a pair, one more lethargic than the other, while the third doorman, the guy who works midnight to eight, makes it a rule never to appear sober in public. Somebody ought to send the three of them up to Eighty-ninth and Riverside for six weeks of basic training.

As I crossed the lobby, a woman got up from the floral-pattern wing chair. She looked to be around twenty-eight. A mane of loose black curls fell a few inches past her shoulders. Her face was an inverted triangle, tapering past a small mouth to a sharp chin. Her mouth was glossy with scarlet lipstick, her eyes deeply shadowed, and if her lashes were natural she must have stimulated their growth with heavy doses of chemical fertilizers.

She said, "Mr. Rhodenbarr? I got to see you."

Well, that explained Armand's greeting. It was his subtle

120

way of fingering me. I hoped he'd been richly rewarded for this service, because he'd just managed to work his way off my Christmas list.

"Well," I said.

"It's kind of important. Would it be okay if we went upstairs? Like to your place?"

She batted her improbable lashes at me. Above them, two narrow curved lines replaced the brows God had given her. If thine eyebrow offend thee, pluck it out.

She looked like a masochist's dream as interpreted by the fevered pen of an adolescent cartoonist. Spike-heeled black shoes with ankle straps. Black wet-look vinyl pants that fitted like paint. A blood-red blouse of some shiny synthetic fabric, tight and clingy enough to prevent one's forgetting even momentarily that human beings are mammals.

A rolled red-and-black umbrella. A black wet-look vinyl purse, a perfect match for the pants. Gold teardrop earrings. The emeralds we'd taken from Colcannon and sold to Abel might look splendid dangling from those little lobes, I thought, and wondered if she'd like me to go back and fetch them for her.

"My place," I said.

"Could we?"

"Why not?"

We ascended in the elevator, and in its confined space I got a full dose of her perfume. There was a lot of musk in it, and some patchouli, and the effect was at once erotic and cheap. I couldn't dismiss the notion that she wasn't really wearing perfume, that she had been born smelling like that.

The elevator reached my floor. The door opened. We walked down the narrow hallway and I imagined that all my neighbors were at their doors, eyes pressed to their peepholes, for a glimpse of what the resident burglar had brought home for the night. As we passed Mrs. Hesch's door, I fancied I could hear her going *tssst-tssst* in reproach.

We hadn't talked in the elevator and we didn't talk in the

hallway. I felt like showing off by opening my door without a key. I restrained myself and unlocked my several locks in the conventional fashion. Inside, I bustled around switching on lamps and wishing I'd changed the sheets since Denise's visit. Not that my guest looked likely to object to rolling around in a bed where another woman had lately lain, but—

"How about a drink?" I suggested. "What can I fix you?"

"Nothing."

"Cup of coffee? Tea, either herb tea or tea tea?"

She shook her head.

"Well, have a seat. Might as well make yourself comfortable. And I don't think I know your name."

I don't think I've ever felt less suave but there didn't seem to be anything I could do about it. She was tacky and obvious and completely irresistible, and I couldn't recall ever having been so thoroughly turned on in my life. I had to fight the urge to get down on my hands and knees and chew the carpet.

She didn't sit down, nor did she tell me her name. Her face clouded for an instant, and she lowered her eyes and reached into her purse.

Her hand came out with a gun in it.

"You son of a bitch," she said. "Stay right where you are, you son of a bitch, or I'll blow your fucking head off."

Fourteen

I stayed right where I was, and she stayed right where she was, and the gun stayed right where it was. In her hand, wobbling a little but not a lot, and pointed straight at me.

It didn't look like a cannon. The guns that get pointed at fictional detectives always look like cannons, and the holes in their muzzles are said to resemble caverns. This gun was undeniably small, just the right size proportionally for her small hand. The latter, I noted now, was a well-shaped hand, its fingernails painted the exact shade of her blouse and her lipstick. And the gun, of course, was black, a flat black automatic pistol with no more than a two-inch barrel. Everything about this lady was red or black. Her favorite birds, I felt certain, were the red-winged blackbird and the scarlet tanager. Her favorite author would have to be Stendhal.

The phone rang. Her eyes flicked toward it, then returned to me. "I'd better answer that," I said.

"You move and I shoot."

"It might be someone important. Suppose it's *Dialing for Dollars*?"

Was it my imagination or had her finger tightened on the

trigger? The phone went on ringing. She was done looking at it, though, and I was incapable of looking at anything but the gun.

I don't like guns. They are cunning little machines crafted exclusively for the purpose of killing people, and it is a purpose I deplore. Guns make me nervous and I do what I can to avoid them, and consequently I don't know a great deal about them. I did know that revolvers have cylinders, which makes them suitable for Russian roulette, whereas automatics, of which my guest's was an example, are generally fitted with safety catches. When engaged, such a device prevents one from depressing the trigger sufficiently to fire the gun.

I could see what might have been a safety catch toward the rear of the gun's muzzle. And I had read enough to know that persons unfamiliar with guns sometimes forget to disengage the safety catch. If I could tell whether the safety was on or off, then perhaps—

"It's loaded," she said. "In case that's what you're wondering."

"I wasn't."

"You're wondering something," she said. Then she said, "Oh," and flicked the safety catch with her thumb. "There. Now don't you try anything, you understand?"

"Sure. If you could just point that thing somewhere else—"

"I don't want to shoot somewhere else. I want to be able to shoot you." ·

"I wish you wouldn't say that." The phone had stopped ringing. "I don't even know you. I don't even know your name."

"What difference does it make?"

"I just—"

"It's Marilyn."

"That's a step." I tried my winningest smile. "I'm Bernie."

124

"I know who you are. You still don't know who I am, do you?"

"You're Marilyn."

"I'm Marilyn Margate."

"Not the actress?"

"What actress?"

I shrugged. "I don't know. The way you said your name I thought you expected me to recognize it. I don't. Do you suppose it's possible you've got the wrong Bernard Rhodenbarr? I know it's not a very common name but there might be more than one of us. My name is Bernard *Grimes* Rhodenbarr, Grimes was my mother's maiden name, like Bouvier or Flanders, so—"

"You son of a bitch."

"Did I say something wrong?"

"You bastard. Bouvier. Flanders. You killed Wanda." This time it wasn't my imagination; her finger definitely tightened on the trigger. And the thing was finally beginning to look like a cannon, and its mouth like the black hole of Calcutta.

"Look," I said, "you're making a terrible mistake. I've never killed anybody in my life. It bothers me to step on a cockroach. I'm the guy who taught Gandhi how to be nonviolent. Compared to me, Albert Schweitzer was a mad-dog killer. I—"

"Shut up."

I shut up.

She said, "You don't know who I am, do you? I thought my last name would tip you off. Rabbit Margate is my brother."

"Rabbit Margate."

"Right."

"I don't know who that is."

"George Edward Margate, but everybody calls him Rabbit. They arrested him this afternoon and charged him with burglary and murder. They say he killed Wanda Tuesday night. My brother never killed anybody."

"Neither did I. Look—"

"Shut up. Either you killed her or you know who did. And you're gonna cop to it. You think I'm letting my kid brother go up for a murder he didn't commit? The hell I am. Either you're gonna confess or I'm gonna shoot you dead."

The phone rang again. She didn't pay any attention to it, and I didn't pay it much mind myself beyond idly wondering who it might be. Was it my caller of a few minutes ago? Was it the person whose call I'd failed to answer when I went out to dinner? Was it the one who'd hung up on me, or the one of the night before who wanted to buy the V-Nickel? Or all of the above, or none of the above?

I decided it didn't matter much, and the ringing stopped, and I said, "George Edward Margate. Rabbit Margate. So you're Rabbit's sister Marilyn."

"Then you *do* know him!"

"Nope. Never heard the name until tonight. But now I know who he is. He's the one who hit the Colcannon place Tuesday and left the radio on."

"You were there. You just admitted it."

"And Rabbit was there. Wasn't he?"

Her expression was wary. "Where do you get off asking the questions? You're not the cops."

"No, I'm not. I'm not the killer, either. I didn't kill anyone Tuesday night. And neither did your brother."

"You're saying he didn't do it."

"That's right. He didn't. He burgled the place, though, didn't he? He went in through the skylight in the bedroom. Was he all by himself?"

"No. Wait a minute. You don't get to ask me questions, for chrissake. I don't have to say he was there and I don't have to say he was with somebody."

"You don't have to say anything. It's all right, Marilyn.

Rabbit didn't kill anybody." I took a breath. It seemed like a good time for disarming candor. "*I* was there," I said, "after Rabbit and his partner had come and gone. The Colcannons weren't home when they burgled the place, and they weren't back yet when I was there, either."

"You can't prove that."

"Nobody can prove I was there in the first place, either. And I *can* prove I didn't meet the Colcannons, because Herbert Colcannon had a nice long look at me through a one-way mirror the other morning and he couldn't identify me."

She nodded slowly. "That's what they said, that there was another suspect named Rhodenbarr but he was cleared because Colcannon hadn't seen him before. But he identified Rabbit and I know he never saw Rabbit, so I thought maybe it was a mistake or you paid somebody off or something. I don't even *know* what I thought. All I knew was my brother was in trouble for something he didn't do, and I figured if I got the person who really did it—"

"But I'm not that person, Marilyn."

"Then who is?"

"I don't know."

"Neither do I, and—" She broke off abruptly and looked at the gun in her hand as if wondering how it had gotten there. "It's loaded," she said.

"I figured it was."

"I almost shot you. I wanted to. As if shooting you would solve everything for Rabbit."

"It would have solved everything for me. But not in a positive way."

"Yeah. Look, I—"

Knock knock knock!

No question who was knocking this time. I cautioned Marilyn with a finger to my lips, then approached her and put those same lips inches from her gold teardrop earring. "Cops," I whispered. I pointed to the bathroom door and she didn't waste time asking questions. She scooted for the bathroom, gun in hand, and she was just closing the door as my latest unannounced guest repeated his knocking.

I asked who it was. "It's who you thought it was, Bern. Open the door, huh?"

I unlocked my locks and admitted Ray Kirschmann. He was wearing the same suit he'd worn yesterday, and now it was wet, which didn't improve the fit any. "Rain," he said heavily, and removed his hat, holding it so that all the water which had collected in the brim could spill onto my floor.

"Thanks," I said.

"Huh?"

"I've had this problem with the floorboards drying out. I was hoping somebody'd come along and water them. What you could do sometime, Ray, is you could call first."

"I did. Line was busy."

"Funny. I wasn't on the phone." Maybe he'd tried while someone else was ringing. "What brings you?"

"The goodness of my heart," he said. "These days I been doin' you nothin' but favors. Drivin' you to your store twice. And stoppin' in tonight to let you know you're in the clear on the Colcannon job. They already got one of the guys who did it."

"Oh?"

He nodded. "Guy named George Margate. Young guy, but he's got a pretty good sheet on him already. Two, three busts for B and E. Never roughed anybody up before, but you know the young ones. They're not what you'd call stable. Maybe his partner was a rough piece of work, or maybe they had drugs in 'em. We found a Baggie full of marijuana in his refrigerator."

"The killer weed."

"Yeah. The marijuana's not what hangs him. It's what else we found at his place. He's been livin' in two rooms on Tenth Avenue in the Forties, maybe a block and a half from the tenement he grew up in. Hell's Kitchen, except you're supposed to call it Clinton now so's people'll forget it's a slum. We tossed his two rooms and he's got half of Colcannon's house packed away there. Silver, Jesus, he had a whole service for twelve in sterling plus all of these bowls and platters. Worth a fortune."

"I remember when it was hardly worth stealing," I said nostalgically. "Then it went from a dollar twenty-nine an ounce to forty dollars an ounce. I remember when *gold* was less than that."

"Yeah. Found some furs, too. Floor-length ranch mink, marten jacket, something else I don't remember. Straight off the list we had from Colcannon, right down to the furriers' labels. All told, we found better'n half of what Colcannon reported as missin', plus some stuff he never listed, because who's got a complete inventory of everythin' right at his fingertips? We figure they split the loot down the middle and the other half's at the partner's place, unless they fenced it already."

"Who's the partner?"

"We don't know yet. He'll tell us when he dopes out that it's the only way he's gonna pull short time, but right now he's James Cagney in every prison movie you ever saw."

"How did you get on to him, Ray?"

"Usual way. Somebody snitched. Maybe he was braggin' in the bars, or just lookin' good and showin' a lot of money, and somebody took two an' two an' put 'em together. Neighborhood he lives in, every third person on the street is a snitch, and the Colcannon job was close to home. What was it, a mile away? Mile and a half?"

I nodded. "Well," I said, "thanks for dropping by to tell me, Ray. I appreciate it."

"Actually," he said, "it's like the other day. I mostly came by to use your bathroom."

"It's out of order."

"Oh yeah?" He went on walking toward the door. "Sometimes these things fix themselves, you know? Or maybe I can fix it for you. I had an uncle was a plumber, showed me a thing or two some years back."

Had she locked the door? I held my breath and he tried the knob and it was locked.

"Door's stuck," he said.

"Must be the weather."

"Yeah, there's a lot of that goin' around. Old retired burglar like yourself, Bern, you oughta be able to get the door open for me."

"A man loses his touch."

"Isn't that just the truth." He walked from the bathroom door to my window and gazed out through the gloom. "I bet you could see the Trade Center," he said, "if the weather was half decent."

"You could."

"And old Abel Crowe got to look over at Jersey all the time. I swear the crooks all get picture-book views. What I get from my window is a close-up of Mrs. Houlihan's washline. You know what I keep wantin' to do, Bern, is tie up Colcannon and Crowe. We got no leads on Crowe, see. Nobody knows nothin'."

"What does Rabbit know about Abel?" Oh, God, why was I calling him that?

"Rabbit?" He frowned, blinked. "I told you, he's Cagney playin' tough. I don't think he ever heard the name, but he's got a partner, right? Even if we don't know who it is."

"So?"

"What you could tell me, Bern, is would anybody try to peddle jewels and silver to Abel Crowe?"

I thought about it, or tried to look as though that was what I was doing. "Abel never took furs," I said. "Stamps, coins, jewelry—that was his field. Silver? Oh, if I found myself with a Revere tankard on my hands, Abel was one of several men I might have offered it to. But garden-variety silver? He'd have had no interest in it. Of course it might be different since silver shot up in price, but who in his right mind would need

130

a fence for it now? You just take it to any of those places where they buy silver by weight for the melting pot. Or you let somebody with a legitimate front do it for you, if you're afraid you'll have trouble cashing a check. You don't need a fence. No, I can't see anybody taking bulk silver to Abel."

"Yeah, that's about what I figured. Who's in your bathroom, Bern?"

"Greta Garbo."

"She wanted to be alone, huh?"

"That's what she told me."

"Well, I don't figure she'd lie about somethin' like that. Anymore'n you'd lie about it. I know she's not the same woman who was here the other night. No cigarettes in the ashtrays. And this is a different perfume. I didn't smell it here before tonight."

"It's, uh, getting late, Ray."

"Uh-huh. It never does get earlier, does it? What did you get out of Colcannon's safe, Bern?"

"I never got into it."

"He listed a couple things that were in the safe. A watch and some jewelry. Earrings, I think it was. They didn't turn up at Margate's. Be funny if we found them up on Riverside Drive, wouldn't it?"

"I don't know what you're getting at."

"I'll tell you, Bern, half the time I don't know myself. All I do is poke around and see where it gets me. Like doin' a jigsaw puzzle by trial and error, pickin' up different pieces and tryin' 'em this way an' that an' seein' what works an' what doesn't."

"It must be fascinating."

"Uh-huh. How'd you come to know Margate?"

"I didn't. Those two puzzle pieces don't fit."

"No? I coulda sworn they did. Then how'd you happen to know they call him Rabbit?"

"That's what you called him, Ray."

"I don't think so. I think I called him George."

"Right, the first time you referred to him. Then there was another time when you called him Rabbit."

He shook his head. "I still don't think so. I think I made a point of it not to call him Rabbit just to see if you would."

"Your tongue must have slipped."

"Somebody's did." He took his hat off, adjusted the brim, put it back on his head. "Well, time I got myself home. You can let the little lady out of the bathroom, Bern. This day an' age, it makes you wonder what she's got to be shy about. But that's just a cop talkin'. This line of work, you're suspicious all the time." He sighed. "Burglars and fences, they got the beautiful views and all. And the women. The only woman you'll find in my bathroom is my wife, and when I look out the window if I don't see Mrs. Houlihan's wash then what I see is Mrs. Houlihan, and between the two I'd as soon look at the laundry. It's no bargain, let me tell you."

"I can imagine."

"I figured you could. What I'd hate to see, Bern, is for you to take a fall for Colcannon. If they already got Rabbit, why should you do time for it? Know what I mean?"

I didn't say anything.

"An' if I can come out with something for my troubles, maybe I can forget some of the things I happened to pick up on. Know what I mean, Bern?"

I knew what he meant.

I locked up after Ray left. Then I stood at the door for a long moment, unlocked the locks, and opened the door far enough to afford me a view of the hallway clear to the elevators. Unless he'd gotten cute enough to duck around a corner, he was gone.

So I locked up again and went over to the bathroom door and told Marilyn the coast was clear.

She had heard most of it. We talked, and by the time we were done she seemed to believe that I'd had nothing to do with the murder of Wanda Colcannon. But she knew Rabbit was equally innocent of murder and she wanted to get him off the hook.

I said, "What about the partner? How many guys did Rabbit work with?"

"Just one."

"Do you know who he was?"

"I don't know if I should say."

"Well, I'm not going to tell anybody. And the police probably already know who he is, if they don't have him in custody by now."

"Rabbit wouldn't fink."

"He might," I said. "Mostly people will, sooner or later. But even if Rabbit's the toughest nut since G. Gordon Liddy, the cops'll probably get the partner the same way they got Rabbit. Some neighborhood snitch'll add two and two and call the cops."

"Why do you want to know who it was?"

"Because maybe he split with Rabbit and went back alone for another try at the safe. Or with a third person."

"Oh." She put a finger to her pointed chin. Her eyes, I noted, didn't need all that makeup. They were large enough without it. "I don't think Harlan would do that," she said.

"Harlan?"

"Harlan Reese. They pulled it off together. If Harlan went back—no, I don't think he would do that, not without telling Rabbit."

"Maybe they both went back."

"You still think Rabbit killed her."

"I didn't say that. But how do you know what Harlan might have done?"

"Rabbit didn't go back a second time. I'm positive of that."

I let it go. We talked about the Third Burglars Carolyn and I had hypothesized, and as I explained the theory it seemed as difficult to pin down as the elusive Third Murderer in *Macbeth*. A couple of roaming vandals, skipping idly over the rooftops in search of loot, happening by chance on a smashed skylight, dropping in for criminous purposes, and committing a slight case of homicide on their way out.

Earlier, I had believed all that. Now it struck me as occupying a rung on the plausibility ladder somewhere between the Great Pumpkin and the Tooth Fairy.

Because Ray was right, albeit for all the wrong reasons. Somehow the two murders, Crowe and Colcannon, were connected. And the only way Rabbit Margate was going to beat a murder rap was by someone's coming up with the real killer, and the police couldn't possibly do that because they already figured they had the real killer, so why look elsewhere?

And if Rabbit didn't wind up in the clear, I was in trouble. Because Rabbit's sister knew I'd been at the Colcannon place after her brother left it, and Ray knew I had heard of Rabbit before he'd mentioned him, and Ray figured there was a connection between me and Colcannon and me and Crowe, and sooner or later he'd do something with his suspicions.

For one thing, he might give Abel's place a really thorough toss of the sort I'd given it, and while I didn't think he'd find the money in the telephone or the rare stamps in the books, neither did I think he'd miss the watch and earrings that were hidden beneath the cigars. Once he found them he'd almost certainly order the place swept for prints again.

And then I'd be in trouble. They had already dusted for prints after Abel's body was found, which was why I hadn't encumbered myself with gloves on my recent visit, that and the fact that I, uh, hadn't thought to bring a pair with me. So my prints were now all over the damned apartment, and while that might not be evidence of homicide (since the prints hadn't been there for the first inspection), it would be very powerful evidence indeed that I'd paid Abel a visit *after* his death, and how was I going to explain that one?

I picked up the phone and called Carolyn. No answer. I called Denise and learned from Jared that she had not come home yet. There was something seriously wrong with telephones, I decided, because I kept calling people and people kept calling me and nobody ever got to talk with anyone else. My life was turning into a clumsy metaphor for the failure of communications in the Age of Alienation.

I dialed 246-4200. It rang and was answered, and for a minute or so I listened without saying a word. Then I replaced the receiver and turned to Marilyn, who was looking at me oddly.

"You didn't say anything," she said.

"That's true. I'm going to help you."

"How?"

"By getting them to release Rabbit."

"How can you do that?"

"By finding out who the Third Burglar was. By learning who really killed Wanda Colcannon."

I was afraid she'd ask how I was going to bring that off, and I would have been stuck for an answer. Instead she asked why.

"That last call I made," I said. "It was Dial-a-Prayer."

"Very funny."

"I'm serious. The prayer today was something like, 'Oh Lord, let me do something today I have never done before. Show me a new way in which I can be of service to a fellow human being.' There was more to it than that, but that's the gist of it."

She raised her penciled eyebrows. "Dial-a-Prayer," she said.

"Call it yourself if you don't believe me."

"And that's why you're going to help Rabbit."

"It's a reason. Won't it do?"

"Yeah," she said. "I guess it will. I guess it'll have to."

Fifteen

Marilyn wanted to leave right away. She had to see a lawyer about getting Rabbit out on bail, which might or might not be possible, and she said something about getting in touch with Harlan Reese. Then, when I warned her that Ray Kirschmann might be lurking in the lobby or laying doggo across the street, she reversed direction completely.

"Oh, God," she said. "Maybe what I oughta do is stay right here."

I looked at her, a veritable vision in *rouge et noir,* and I inhaled her scent, and I listened with amazement to my very own voice telling her I didn't think that was a good idea. "You have things to do," I said, "and *I* have things to do, and we'd better go do them. Besides, Ray could turn ornery and come back with a warrant and a crowbar, and then the bathroom wouldn't be sacrosanct anymore. One thing, though. Maybe you should leave the gun here."

She shook her head. "It doesn't belong to me. My boss keeps it in case we get held up. I think she just likes having it, you know? I mean who's gonna hold up a beauty parlor?"

"Is that where you work?"

She nodded. "Hair Apparent. There's four operators plus Magda, she's the owner. I'm working tomorrow. I'll put the gun back then."

"Good. Because if the police found it in your purse—"

"I know."

We were in the hallway and I was locking the last of the locks when the phone started ringing. I gritted my teeth. If I unlocked everything and raced I still wouldn't get to the phone on time, and if I did it would just be somebody offering me free home delivery of the Newark *Star-Ledger.* The hell with it.

The elevator took us down past the lobby to the basement. We went through the laundry room and down a dimly lit corridor to the service entrance. I held the door for her and she climbed a short flight of stairs, opened her red-and-black umbrella, and disappeared into the night.

Back in my apartment, I stood for a moment glaring at my phone and wondering how many times it had rung while I was letting Marilyn out. It wasn't ringing now, and it was getting late enough to discourage me from placing many calls of my own. I tried one, dialing Carolyn's number, and wasn't surprised when nobody answered.

The four little cups of espresso were starting to wear off and I poured myself a healthy hooker of straight Scotch to speed them on their way. I drank it down, then got a taller glass from the cupboard and stirred an ounce or two of Scotch into four or five ounces of milk. The perfect nightcap —the milk coats your stomach while the Scotch rots your liver.

The phone rang.

I leaped for it, then made myself draw a calming breath before lifting the receiver to my ear. A male voice, one I'd last heard almost twenty-two hours ago, said, "Rhodenbarr? I want the nickel."

"Who doesn't?"

"What do you mean?"

"Everybody wants it. I wouldn't mind getting my own hands on it."

"Don't joke with me. I know you have the coin."

"I had it. I don't have it anymore."

There was a pause, and for a moment I thought I'd lost him. Then he said, "You're lying."

"No. Do you think I'm crazy enough to pop it in the same pocket as the keys and the Saint Christopher medal? I wouldn't do that, and I wouldn't keep it around the house, either. Not with all the burglaries you hear about in this town."

This last didn't win a chuckle. "You have access to the coin?"

"It's where I can get it."

"Get it now," he urged. "And name your price and we will arrange a meeting. I have the rest of the night at my disposal, and—"

"I'm afraid I can't say the same," I said. "If I don't get enough sleep I'm a terrible grouch the next day. Anyway, I couldn't get hold of the coin at this hour even if I wanted to, which I don't. I'm afraid it'll have to be tomorrow."

"What time tomorrow?"

"That's hard to say. Give me a number where I can reach you."

This time I got the chuckle. "I think not, Rhodenbarr. It will be better if I continue to call you. Estimate how much time you'll need to gain possession of the coin, then return to your apartment at an appointed hour and I'll telephone you. Merely tell me the hour."

In other words, be at a specific place at a specific time with the coin in my hand. "Inconvenient," I said. "Tell you what. There's another number where I'll be tomorrow afternoon at two."

"And the number?"

I gave him Carolyn's. She sublets her rent-controlled apartment from a man named Nathan Aranow, and as he remains the tenant of record her phone is listed in his name. (Half the people in New York operate this way. The other half pay $500 a month for a studio apartment.) I didn't think he could get the name and address from the number, and if he did how was he going to find Nathan Aranow? Carolyn simply mailed a money order in that name to her landlord every month. For all any of us knew, Nathan Aranow had been wiped out years ago in a flash flood.

He repeated the number. "And the coin," he said. "Who else knows you have it?"

"Nobody."

"You had no accomplice?"

"I always work alone."

"And you haven't spoken to anyone?"

"I've spoken to plenty of people, but not about the coin."

"So no one else knows you have it."

"As far as I know," I said, "nobody else even knows it's missing. Just you and I and Herbert Franklin Colcannon, unless he's told somebody, and I don't think he has." Or else Ray Kirschmann would have been sniffing after half a million dollars, and if that had been the case he'd have been drooling all over my rug. "He might not report it, not if it wasn't insured. And if he had reasons."

"I'm sure he didn't report it."

"Of course Rabbit might talk."

"Rabbit?"

"George Edward Margate. Isn't that why you fingered the Colcannon place for him? You should have picked someone who knew how to punch a safe. I guess the nickel was supposed to be your finder's fee for setting up the job."

A long low chuckle. "Clever," he said. "I should have made my arrangements with you in the first place."

"You certainly should have. It might help if I knew your name."

"It might," he said. "I'll call you tomorrow at two o'clock. That number's in the Village, isn't it?"

"I own a bookstore on East Eleventh Street. There's two phones, one listed and one unlisted. I gave you the number of the unlisted one."

"Shall I simply meet you at your store, then?"

"No," I said. "Call the number at two."

I hung up and returned to my Scotch and milk. The milk was warmish, but that's supposed to be an advantage when you're trying to go to sleep. I sat down and sipped and thought that I'd done rather a lot of lying. Well, Dial-a-Prayer hadn't said anything provocative about honesty. Just being of service to one's fellow man, and if I wasn't that, then what was I?

The phone rang. I picked it up and it was Carolyn. "Been calling you all night," she said. "What the hell happened to you, Bernie? Either nobody answered or the line was busy, or once in a while I would get a wrong number. What's been happening?"

"Everything."

"Are you gonna have to get glasses?"

"Glasses?"

"Didn't you say you were going to the eye doctor?"

"Oh. Yeah, right."

"You have to get glasses?"

"No, but he said I should stop reading in the dark."

"I could have told you that. You okay? You sound a little funny."

She sounded about half lit, but I didn't bother to mention it. "I'm fine," I said. "Just exhausted. A lot of things have happened but I can't really talk now."

"Company?"

"Yes," I said, and then it struck me that I'd better stop this lying before my nose started to grow. "No," I said.

"I knew it was one or the other. But which?"

"I'm alone," I said, "but I evidently can't think straight. Are you at home?"

"No, I'm bopping around the bars. Why?"

"Going back to your place later?"

"Unless I get lucky, which it doesn't look like I'm gonna. Why?"

"You'll be home in the morning? Or will you be at the Poodle Factory?"

"I don't work Saturdays anymore, Bernie. I don't have to, not since I started doing a little burglary to make ends meet. Remember?"

"Maybe you could go over to the store when you wake up," I said, "and pick up your telephone answering machine, and take it back to your apartment."

"Why would I want to do that?"

"I'll be over around ten or so and tell you all about it."

"Jesus, I certainly hope so."

I hung up and it rang again and it was Denise, home at last and returning my call. I asked her how she would like company around one-thirty.

"It's almost that now," she said.

"I mean tomorrow afternoon. All right if I drop in for a few minutes?"

"Sure. Just for a few minutes?"

"Maybe an hour at the outside."

"Sure, I guess. Does this mark a new development in our ever-evolving relationship, Bernie? Are you advance-booking a quickie or something?"

"No," I said. "I'll be over around one-thirty, maybe a quarter of two, and I'll explain everything."

"I can hardly wait."

I hung up and got undressed. When I took my socks off I sat for a moment on the edge of my bed and examined my feet. I had never really studied them before, and it had certainly never occurred to me that they were narrow. They definitely looked narrow now, long and skinny and foolish. And there was no question about it, my second toes extended beyond my big toes. I tried to retract the offending second toes, tried to extend the big toes, but this didn't work, and I must have been damned tired to think it might.

Morton's Foot. I had it, all right, and while it wasn't as dismaying as a positive Wassermann, I can't say I felt happy about it.

So the phone rang.

I picked it up. A woman with an English accent said, "I beg your pardon?"

"Huh?"

"Is this Bernard Rhodenbarr?"

"Yes."

"I thought I might have dialed the weather report by mistake. You said 'It never rains but it pours.'"

"I didn't realize I'd said that aloud."

"You did, actually, and it *is* raining, and—I'm sorry to be calling you so late. I couldn't reach you earlier. My name is Jessica Garland. I don't know if that means anything to you."

"Not offhand, but I don't think my mind's at its sharpest. Not if I'm capable of answering the phone with a code phrase from a spy movie."

"You know, it did rather sound like that. I thought my grandfather might have mentioned me, Mr. Rhodenbarr."

"Your grandfather?"

"Abel Crowe."

My jaw may have hung loose for a moment. Then I said, "I never knew Abel had a grandchild. I never even knew he'd been married."

"I don't know that he was. He was certainly never married to my grandmother. She was from Budapest originally, and the two of them were lovers in Vienna before the war. When the Nazis annexed Austria in '38 she got out with my mother

142

in her arms and the clothes she was wearing and nothing else. Grandfather's parting gift to her was a small fortune in rare stamps which she concealed in the lining of her coat. She went from Vienna to Antwerp, where she sold the stamps, and from there to London, where she died in the Blitz. Grandfather wound up in a concentration camp and survived."

"And your mother—?"

"Mother was five or six years old when Grandmother was killed. She was taken in by a neighbor family and grew up as an English girl. She married young, had me early on, and assumed her own father was dead, that he'd died in a concentration camp or in the war. It must have been about six years ago that she learned otherwise. I say, I'm doing a great lot of talking, aren't I? Do you mind terribly?"

"I find it rather soothing."

"Do you? Well, Grandfather literally turned up on our doorstep in Croydon. It seems he'd hired agents and finally succeeded in tracing Mother. There was a joyful reunion, but before very long they found themselves with precious little to say to each other. She'd grown up to be a rather ordinary English suburban housewife, while Grandfather—well, you know the sort of life he led."

"Yes."

"He returned to the States. He wrote letters, but they were more to me and my brother than to Mum. I've a younger brother, you see. Two years ago Grandfather wrote suggesting I might care to try living in America, and the suggestion came at just the right time. I quit my hateful job, said goodbye to my dreary young man, and boarded one of Freddie Laker's DC-10's. And to make a long story short—do you know, when people say 'To make a long story short,' it's already too late. In any event, I've been here ever since."

"In New York?"

"In Brooklyn, actually. Do you know Cobble Hill?"

"Sort of."

"I lived at first in a women's residential hotel in Gramercy Park. Then I moved here. The job at which I work is not hateful, and the young man with whom I live is not at all dreary, and I'm hardly ever homesick, actually. I'm rambling all over the lot, aren't I? Chalk it up to exhaustion, physical and emotional. And there's a point to all this, actually."

"I felt sure there would be."

"How very trusting of you. The point is that Grandfather spoke of you, and not only as, oh, shall we say a business associate?"

"I guess we shall."

"But also as a friend, don't you see. And now he's dead, as of course you know, and I shall miss him, and I think it's quite horrid how he died and I hope they catch the person responsible, but in the meantime it rather falls to me to get everything in order. I don't know what he would have wanted in the line of funeral arrangements because he never talked about the possibility of his own death, unless he left a letter of some sort, and if so it hasn't come to light yet. And of course the police have the body at the morgue and I don't know when they're likely to release it. When they do I suspect I'll manage some sort of private funeral without any ceremony, but in the meantime I think it would be fitting to have some sort of memorial service, don't you?"

"I guess that would be nice."

"I've arranged something, actually. There'll be a service at the Church of the Redeemer on Henry Street between Congress and Amity Streets. That's here in Cobble Hill. Do you know where it is?"

"I'll be able to find it."

"It's the only church I could find that would allow a memorial service on a Sunday. We'll be meeting there that afternoon at two-thirty. The service won't be religious because Grandfather wasn't a religious man. He did have a

144

spiritual side, however. I don't know if he ever showed that side to you."

"I know the sort of reading he did."

"Yes, all the great moral philosophers. I told them at the church that we'd conduct our own service. Clay, the chap I live with, is going to read something. He was quite fond of Grandfather. And I'll probably read something myself, and I thought you might be able to take part in the service, Mr. Rhodenbarr."

"Call me Bernie. Yes, I could probably find something to read. I'd like to do that."

"Or just say a few words, or both. As you choose." She hesitated. "There's another thing, actually. I saw Grandfather every few weeks and we were close in certain ways, but he didn't mention many of his . . . business friends. I know you were a friend of his, and I know of one or two others in that category, but perhaps you'll be able to think of some other persons who might properly come to the service."

"It's possible."

"Would you just go ahead and invite anyone you think ought to be invited? May I just leave that up to you?"

"All right."

"I've already spoken to several of the people in his building, and one woman's going to post a notice in the lobby. I suppose I should have made arrangements with a church in that neighborhood. Some of those people find it difficult to get around easily. But I'd already made plans with the Church of the Redeemer before I thought of it. I hope they won't mind coming all the way out to Brooklyn."

"Perhaps it'll be an adventure for them."

"I just hope the weather's decent. The rain's expected to have left off by then, but the weatherman doesn't give guarantees, does he?"

"Not as a general rule."

"No, more's the pity. I'm sorry to have gone on so, Mr. Rhodenbarr, but—"

"Bernie."

"Bernie. It's late and I'm tired, perhaps more so than I'd realized. You will try to come? Sunday at two-thirty? And you'll invite anyone you think of?"

"Definitely," I said. "And I'll bring along something to read."

I wrote down the time and the address and the name of the church. Carolyn would want to come, of course. Anybody else?

I got in bed and tried to think if I knew anyone who'd want to attend a memorial service for Abel. I wasn't acquainted with many other burglars, having a longstanding preference for the company of law-abiding citizens, and I didn't know who Abel's friends were. Would Ray Kirschmann want to make the trip? I thought about it and decided that he might.

My mind drifted around. So Abel had a granddaughter. How old was Jessica Garland likely to be? Her mum must have been born in 1936 or thereabouts, and if she had indeed married young and had Jessica early on, then twenty-four or twenty-five sounded like a reasonable ballpark figure. I didn't have any trouble picturing Abel playing host to a young woman about that age, telling her charming lies about the old days in the Viennese coffeehouses, plying her with strudel and eclairs.

And he'd never once mentioned her, the old fox.

I was almost asleep when a thought nudged me back awake again. I got out of bed, looked up a number, made a phone call. It rang four times before a man answered it.

I stayed as silent as if I'd called Dial-a-Prayer. I listened, and the man who'd answered said *"Hello?"* several times, querulously, while in the background music played and a dog interposed an occasional bark. Then he hung up—the man, I trust, rather than the dog—and I went back to bed.

146

Sixteen

One of the things I'd found time to do between late phone calls was set my alarm clock, and come morning it rang its fool head off. I got up and groped my way through a shower and a shave and the first cup of coffee, then turned on the radio and toasted a couple slices of whole-grain bread, buttered them, jammed them, ate them, drank some more coffee, drew the drapes and cocked an eye at the dawn.

It looked promising, even to a cocked eye. To the east, dark clouds still obscured the newly risen sun. But the sky was clear in the west, and the winds generally blow from that direction, sweeping yesterday's weather out over the Atlantic —which, in this case, was right where it belonged. The sky over the Hudson had a distinctly blue cast to it.

I poured myself one more cup of coffee, settled in my most nearly comfortable chair with the phone and the phone book, glanced ruefully at Morton's feet, and let my fingers do the walking.

My first call was to the American Numismatic Society, located some four miles north of me at Broadway and 156th Street. I introduced myself as James Klavin of the New York

Times and explained I was doing a piece on the 1913 V-Nickel. Could he tell me a few things about the coin? Was it true, for example, that only five specimens were known to exist? And did he happen to know where those specimens were located at the present time? Could he say when a specimen had last changed hands? And for what price?

Almost everyone likes to cooperate with the press. Describe yourself as a reporter and you can ask no end of time-consuming and impertinent questions, and all people ask of you in return is that you spell their names right. The man I spoke with, a Mr. Skeffington, said he might be a moment and offered to ring me back. I said I'd hold, and I held for ten minutes, sipping coffee and wiggling my toes, while he scurried around doing my legwork for me.

He came back in due course and told me more than I really needed to know, repeating a lot of what Abel had told us Tuesday night. There were indeed five specimens, four of them in public collections, one in private hands, and he was able to furnish me with the names of the four institutions and the private collector.

He was less helpful on the subject of value. The A.N.S. is a high-minded outfit, more interested in scholarly matters like die varieties and the historical context of numismatics than such crass considerations as price. The most recent cash transaction of which Mr. Skeffington had a record was a sale Abel had mentioned—in 1976, for $130,000. According to Abel there'd been a sale since then for a substantially higher price.

I called the four museums in turn. At the Smithsonian in Washington, the curator of coins and medals was a gentleman with a dry voice and a hyphenated surname. He confirmed that a 1913 V-Nickel was a part of the Smithsonian's numismatic holdings, having been acquired as a gift of Mrs. R. Henry Norweb in 1978.

"It's on permanent display," he informed me, "and it's terribly popular. Tourists gawk at it and tell each other how beautiful it is. Now our coin is a frosty proof, but aside from that it looks like any Liberty Head Nickel, hardly an extraordinary item from the standpoint of numismatic design. You might care to argue that the Standing Liberty Quarter is beautiful, or the Saint-Gaudens high-relief twenty-dollar gold piece, but the Liberty Head Nickel? What makes this example beautiful? The date? Why, it's the value, of course. The rarity, the legends. People *ooh* and *ahh* at diamonds, too, and couldn't tell them from cut glass, not by looking at them. What exactly did you want to know about our coin?"

"I just wanted to make sure it was still there."

A dry chuckle. "Oh, it's still here. We haven't had to spend it yet. Not much you can buy with a nickel nowadays, anyway, so I guess we'll hang onto it for the present."

A woman at the Boston Museum of Fine Arts confirmed that a 1913 V-Nickel was one of the stars of the museum's coin display and had been since its acquisition by bequest shortly after the Second World War. "It's an extremely important numismatic item," she said, sounding like catalogue copy, "and we're gratified to have it here in Boston."

An assistant curator at the Museum of Science and Industry was similarly gratified to have Nickel No. 3 in Cincinnati, where it had reposed since the mid-thirties. "We've deaccessioned a substantial portion of our coin holdings in the past few years," he told me. "We've had budget problems, and the coins have increased so dramatically in value that they seemed to represent a disproportionate amount of our capital in relation to their display value. There's been some pressure on us to eliminate coins altogether, as we did with our stamps, but then our philatelic collection was never more than third-rate. The 1913 Nickel's the star of our show. We've no plans to let it go, not that they've told me about. It's popular, you see, especially with the children. I wouldn't be surprised if someone's looking at it right now."

Nickel No. 4 had belonged to the Museum of the Baltimore Historical Society until a little over a year ago, I learned from a woman whose speech indicated an origin rather further south than Baltimore. "It was our only important coin," she said. "We're really only interested in articles relating to the history of the city of Baltimore, but people tend to will their prize possessions to museums, and we in turn tend to accept what's left to us. We had the nickel for years and years, and of course its value increased, and from time to time there was talk of consigning it to an auction or selling it privately to a fellow institution. Then a foundation in Philadelphia devoted exclusively to numismatics came to us offering to exchange the Copley portrait of Charles Carroll of Carrollton." She went on to explain that Charles Carroll, born in Annapolis, had been a member of the Continental Congress, a signer of the Declaration of Independence, and a United States senator. I already knew who Copley was.

"It was an offah we couldn't refuse," she said solemnly, and I pictured Marlon Brando as Don Corleone, holding a pistol to this Southern belle's head, urging her to swap the nickel for the portrait.

The place in Philadelphia called itself the Gallery of American and International Numismatics, and the man I spoke to gave his name as Milo Hracec, and spelled it for me. He was second in command, he explained; his boss was Howard Pitterman, which name he also spelled, and Pitterman had Saturdays off.

Hracec confirmed that the gallery did indeed own a 1913 Nickel. "It is a part of our type set of United States coinage," he said. "You know what a type set is? One example of each design. Type collecting has become popular as fewer hobbyists can afford to collect complete sets by date and mint mark. Of course that is not the foremost consideration here, because Mr. Ruslander has placed generous funds at the gallery's disposal."

"Mr. Ruslander?"

"Gordon Ruslander of the Liberty Bell Mint. You're probably familiar with their sets of medals for collectors."

I was indeed. Like the Franklin Mint, also in Philadelphia, Liberty Bell specialized in series of contemporary medals which they peddled to collectors by subscription with the intimation that the little silver discs would someday increase in value. They'd always been a drug on the resale market, and on more than one occasion I'd left sets of the medals in their owners' desks, writing them off as not worth stealing. Now, with the surge in the price of silver, the damned things had soared to more than triple their issue price in bullion value.

Ruslander, I was told, had established the Gallery of American and International Numismatics three years previously, donating his own personal collection along with a hefty chunk of cash. And the U.S. type set, in which the 1913 V-Nickel reposed, was the gallery's star attraction.

"In a type set," Hracec explained, "any coin of the type will do. But in the gallery's collection, we strive for the rarest date and mint variety attainable for that type, instead of settling for a common and readily affordable example. In 1873–4, for instance, Liberty Seated Dimes were struck with arrows flanking the date. Uncirculated specimens of the Philadelphia and San Francisco issues range from six or seven hundred to perhaps a thousand or twelve hundred dollars. Our coin is one struck at Carson City, the 1873-CC, and our specimen is superior in quality to the one which sold at a Kagin auction seven years ago for twenty-seven thousand dollars.

"Originally our V-Nickel slot was filled by a proof example of the 1885, the rarest date of the regular series. It's worth perhaps a thousand dollars, a little more than twice the price of common proofs. There was some question as to whether we would even want to have the 1913, since it was not a regularly issued coin, but when we learned the Baltimore

Historical Society might let theirs go, Mr. Ruslander wouldn't rest until we had it. He happened to own a portrait by Copley that he knew they would want—"

And I got to hear about Charles Carroll of Carrollton all over again. On and on it went, and when I was done with Mr. Hracec I had to call Stillwater, Oklahoma, where I spoke with a man named Dale Arnott. Mr. Arnott evidently owned a fair portion of Payne County and ran beef cattle on his land, moving them out of the way now and then to make room for an oil well. He had indeed owned the 1913 V-Nickel, having bought it in '76 for $130,000, and his had been the one resold a year or two ago for $200,000.

"I had my fun with it," he said, "and I got a kick at coin conventions, hauling it out of a pocketful of change and tossing it to match folks for drinks. You'd like to die from the look on their faces. Way I looked at it, a nickel's a nickel, so why not toss it heads or tails?"

"Weren't you worried you'd lower its value?"

"Nope. It wasn't in the best condition to start with, you see. Oh, it's better than extra fine, but the proof surface isn't what it was when they minted it. I guess the other four are in better shape. I saw the one in the Smithsonian Institution once and it was a perfect frosty proof with a mirrorlike field, and mine was nothing like that. So I had my pleasure owning it, and then a fellow offered me a handsome profit on it, and I told him if he'd up his price to an even two hundred thousand he could own himself a five-cent piece. I could give you his name but I don't know as he'd want me doing that."

I asked if the buyer still had the coin.

"'Less he sold it," Arnott said. "You in the market yourself? I could call the gentleman and find out if he wants to sell."

"I'm just a reporter, Mr. Arnott."

"Well, I was thinking that it's easy to be a reporter over the phone. I've been that in my time, and a Baptist minister and any number of lawyers. Now don't let me offend you, sir.

If you want to be a reporter that's just what you are, and if you want to find out if the coin's for sale—"

"I just want to find out if he still owns it. I don't care if it's for sale or not."

"Then you give me a telephone number where you'll be for an hour or so, and I'll see what I can find out."

I gave him Carolyn's.

I made four more calls, to Washington, Boston, Cincinnati and Philadelphia. Then I called the A.N.S. again, and I called *Coin World,* the weekly newspaper in Sidney, Ohio. By the time I was finished my fingers had done so much walking I was beginning to worry about them. After all, my hands were unquestionably narrow—odd I hadn't ever noticed this before. And there was no denying that my index fingers were substantially longer than my thumbs.

The implications were clear enough. I had Morton's Hand, and I knew only too well where that could lead. Pain in the palm. Wrist spurs. Forearm tendinitis. And, sooner or later, the dreaded Dialer's Shoulder.

I hung up and got the hell out of there.

Seventeen

I got to Carolyn's house around noon. I sat there with a cat on my lap and a cup of coffee at my elbow and did what I could to bring my hostess up to date.

I had my work cut out for me. There was a lot of water over the dam or under the bridge or wherever it goes these days, and my task wasn't rendered easier by Carolyn's headache. Another of those dreaded sugar hangovers, no doubt. Maybe the right pair of orthotics would solve everything.

"What I can't get over," she said, "is that you went to Abel's without me."

"We couldn't have both gotten in. And it was risky, and there was nothing two people could do better than one."

"And then you got home from Abel's and didn't say anything."

"I tried, dammit. I kept calling you."

"Bern, I kept calling *you.* Either you were out or the line was busy."

"I know. I kept calling everybody and everybody kept calling me. These things happen. It doesn't matter. We finally reached each other, didn't we?"

"Yeah, last night. And you didn't tell me zip until just now."

"It was too late last night."

"Yeah."

"And there wasn't that much to tell."

"No, not much at all. Just that you got into Abel's apartment and came home and some beautician held a gun on you and accused you of framing her brother for murder."

"That's not exactly what she said."

"I don't really care what she said exactly."

"You're pissed."

"Kind of, yeah."

"Would it help if I apologized?"

"Try it and let's see."

"Well," I said, "I'm sorry, Carolyn. We're partners, and I certainly meant to keep you in the picture, but things got out of control for a little while there. I didn't know if I'd be able to get into Abel's apartment and I just went ahead and did things on my own, figuring I'd catch up with you later. And I'm sorry."

She sat in silence for a moment. Then she said, "Quit it, Ubi," to the Russian Blue, who was scratching the side of the couch. From my lap, Archie purred with unmistakable moral superiority.

"Nope," Carolyn said. "It doesn't help."

"My apology, you mean?"

"Uh-huh. Doesn't do a thing for me. I'm still pissed. But I'll get over it. Who killed Wanda?"

"I'm not sure."

"How about Abel?"

"I'm not sure of that, either."

"Well—"

The phone rang. I moved Archie and answered it, and it was Mr. Arnott calling from Stillwater, Oklahoma. He hadn't reversed the charges, either. I guess people who can pay $130,000 for a nickel don't worry about their phone bills.

"The fellow who bought my nickel wants to remain anonymous," he said. "I couldn't say whether it's burglars or the tax collector he's scared of. Coin's not for sale, though. He's still got it, and he figures to keep it."

"The hell with him," I said. "I think I'd rather buy a painting anyway."

"That way you'll have something you can hang on the wall."

"That's what I decided."

"I didn't figure you was a reporter, not for a minute."

I reported the conversation to Carolyn. "Arnott's coin is still with the mysterious purchaser," I explained. "Anyway, it was a lightly circulated specimen, so it couldn't have been the one we carried from Eighteenth Street to Riverside Drive."

She frowned. "There were five of the nickels altogether."

"Right."

"Now there's one in Washington, one in Boston, one in Cincinnati, one in—Philadelphia?"

"Right."

"And one that your friend in Oklahoma sold to some mystery man. So the mystery man is Colcannon. Except he can't be, because that coin's circulated and Colcannon's was a perfect proof."

"Right."

"So there are five nickels *plus* the Colcannon nickel."

"Right."

"Which Colcannon doesn't have anymore, and which wasn't at Abel's, so we don't know where it is."

"Right."

"Which means the nickel we stole was a counterfeit."

"It's possible."

"But you don't think so?"

"No. I'm positive it's genuine."

"Then there are actually six nickels."

"No. Only five."

156

She sat for a moment, puzzling, then threw her hands in the air. "Bern," she said, "would you for chrissake quit cocking around? My whole head hurts except for the part I normally think with, which is numb. Just explain, will you? Simply, so I can understand it."

I explained. Simply. So she could understand it.

"Oh," she said.

"Does it make sense? Stand up? Hold water?"

"I think so. What about the questions I asked you earlier? There was a Third Burglar who killed Wanda. Do you know who he was?"

"I have an idea."

"And do you have an idea who killed Abel?"

"Sort of. But I can't be sure of it, and I certainly can't prove it, and—"

"Tell me anyway, Bernie."

"I sort of hate to say anything at this stage."

"Why? Because you don't want to spoil the surprise? Bern, if you were really sincere with that apology you gave me a few minutes ago, why don't you prove it?"

I shifted a little on the chair. There are those who might have said I squirmed. "We've got to get out of here," I said. "It may have been a mistake giving out your number. If the man who wants to buy the coin could find out my name and how to reach me, he might have a connection in the Police Department or access to one of the phone company's reverse directories. I don't want us to be where he can get at us. He knows I'm going to be at this phone at two, so—"

"There's time, Bern. You can tell me your theories and we'll still have plenty of time."

Archie extended his forepaws and stretched. "Archie's no name for a cat," I said. "The cat's Mehitabel, remember?"

"He's a boy cat, dum-dum. He's Rex Stout's Archie, not Don Marquis's Archy."

"Oh."

"I could always get a pet cockroach and name her Mehitabel. If I knew it was a girl cockroach. Why am I sitting here talking about cockroaches? You changed the subject, dammit."

"I guess I did."

"Well, change it back again. Who killed Wanda and Abel?"

I gave up and told her.

Afterward we set up the answering machine with a simple message that I recorded, telling whoever called to ring me at Denise's number. I got my attaché case from Carolyn's closet, where it was still keeping the Chagall company. We got out of there and took a cab to the Poodle Factory. We went inside, and when we emerged a couple of minutes later my attaché case was the slightest bit heavier. Carolyn locked up and we caught another cab to the Narrowback Gallery.

On the way there she wanted to know why we had to go to Denise's place. I said I'd already told her, and expressed the wish that the two of them got along better.

"You might as well wish for wings," she said. "Oh, she's all right for a scarecrow, but don't you have better taste than that? There must be an attractive straight woman somewhere in New York. How about Angela?"

"Who?"

"The waitress at the Bum Rap."

"I thought you decided she was gay."

"I decided the question calls for research. Monday I'm gonna ask her a question that'll let me know if she's gay without tipping her off if she isn't."

"What's the question?"

"Something like, 'Angela, how about you and me getting married?'"

"You don't think that's overly subtle?"

"Well, I might work on the phrasing a little."

* * *

Any pleasure Denise might have felt at seeing me was completely obliterated by her reaction to the sight of Carolyn. The dismay showed clearly on her face. "Oh, the dog lady," she said. "I don't seem to remember your name."

"It's Carolyn," I was saying, even as Carolyn was saying, "You can call me Ms. Kaiser." It was going to be a long afternoon, I realized, and I was glad I wasn't going to be on hand for very much more of it.

"I didn't recognize you at first," Denise said. "I didn't remember you as being quite so short as you are, and at first glance I thought you were a child."

"It's my air of innocence that does it," Carolyn said. She stationed herself in front of one of the more striking paintings on display, tilting her head to one side and planting herself with her hands on her hips. "Painting must really be fun when you don't have to make it look like anything," she said. "You can just sort of smear the paint on any old way, can't you?"

"I'll make some coffee," Denise said. "And I'm sure Ms. Kaiser must want something to eat."

"No, I don't think so," Carolyn said. "I haven't had much of an appetite lately. Maybe I'm getting anorexia. I understand it strikes some women late in life."

It went on like this, and I might have been able to sit back and enjoy it if they hadn't both been favorite people of mine. God knows there was nothing else for me to do. They didn't need a referee; they were doing fine all by themselves, and nobody was bothering to keep score. Jared, I learned, was out for the afternoon. I thought that showed sound judgment on his part.

The phone rang at two o'clock. I picked it up, held the receiver to my ear, and waited until I heard a familiar voice. Then I nodded shortly and passed the receiver to Carolyn.

"The gentleman you're calling hasn't arrived yet," she

159

said. "Please call again in precisely fifteen minutes."

She hung up, looked at me. I grabbed up my attaché case and got to my feet. "I'm on my way," I said. "You know what you're supposed to tell him when he calls?"

"Uh-huh. He should go to the Squires coffee shop at the corner of Madison and Seventy-ninth. He should sit at the table furthest from the door and wait, and you'll either join him at his table or have him paged under the name of Madison, as in Avenue."

"And if he asks about the coin—"

"You've got it."

"Right."

"You've got me involved in something," Denise said. "You're still a burglar, aren't you, Bernie? Of course you are. The leopard doesn't change his spots. Or the convict his stripes, apparently."

"They don't wear stripes in prison anymore."

"Oh, but they should. They're so slimming. But you'd know what they wear and don't wear, wouldn't you? You've been there. And you're still a burglar. Are you a killer, too?" She looked at Carolyn. "And what are *you,* exactly? His henchperson?"

"Carolyn will explain everything," I said. And I didn't envy her a bit.

All of a sudden I was taking cabs a lot. I took the third of the day to the corner of Eighteenth Street and Ninth Avenue. We made good time, and by two-fifteen I was staked out across the street from the heavy iron gate marked 442½. At that very moment he was supposed to be on the phone, and perhaps he was, because ten minutes later the gate swung open and Herbert Franklin Colcannon emerged from it. I was in a shadowy doorway where he couldn't have seen me, but he didn't even look in my direction, turning to his left and striding purposefully toward Tenth Avenue, either to catch a cab or because he had a car parked there.

I didn't care which it was. I let him reach the corner, then jogged across the street—I was wearing my Pumas, their excessive width notwithstanding. It was a bright sunny afternoon and there were people on the street, but that didn't bother me this time. I knew which of my skeleton keys would do for the lock on the iron gate, since I'd already determined that Tuesday night, so I had the key in hand as I crossed the street and I was through the gate and had it locked behind me in a matter of seconds.

I wasn't wearing rubber gloves, either. This time around I didn't care about prints. If things went wrong they'd go wrong dramatically, and fingerprints would be the least of my worries. If things went right, nobody would give a damn where my fingers had been.

Once I was through the gate and into the tunnel I unsnapped the locks on my attaché case and took the gun from it.

Nasty things, guns. This one looked to have been made of blued steel, but its surface was warmer to the touch. The material was some sort of high-impact phenolic resin. I suppose I could have carried it onto an airplane. I let my hand accustom itself to the feel of the weapon, checked its load, and made my way through the tunnel.

I wanted that gun in my hand in case Astrid was spending the afternoon in the garden. I didn't expect that would be the case, but the bitch was attack-trained and I wasn't, and I didn't want to be unprepared for an encounter with her. At the mouth of the tunnel I paused with the gun at my side and scanned the garden carefully.

No Astrid. No people, either. I slipped the gun beneath the waistband of my trousers where my jacket would screen it from view and then walked quickly across the flagstone patio with scarcely a glance at the tulips and daffodils, the little fishpond, the semicircular bench.

With a garden like that, why would a man go chasing phantom coins all over the place? Of course it might not be

161

his garden, it might indeed belong to the front house, but surely he could sit in it, couldn't he?

I mounted the stoop and rang the bell. I'd seen him leave, but how did I know he'd been alone there? I put my ear to the door and listened, and I heard some barking that I could have heard without putting my ear to the door, and then a rumbling sound as if something bulky had just fallen down a flight of stairs. A chest of drawers, say, or an excitable Bouvier des Flandres. The barking was repeated and got louder, and all I had between me and Astrid was a wooden door about two inches thick.

Which I promptly set about opening.

The locks had been easy the first time, and they're always easier the second time around. My fingers remembered their inner workings, and I knocked them off one-two-three in not many more seconds than it takes to tell about it. If anyone had watched from a rear window of the front house, say, I don't think he'd have had cause for suspicion.

I turned the knob, opened the door the merest fraction of an inch. The barking increased in volume and climbed in pitch. There was a manic intensity in it now—or perhaps it just sounded that way to me.

I drew the gun, checked the load once more.

Was there any way I could avoid doing this? Couldn't I just close the door and lock up after myself and get the hell out? Maybe I could rush up to Madison and Seventy-ninth, maybe Colcannon and I could work something out, maybe—

Quit stalling, Rhodenbarr.

I leveled the gun in my right hand, held the doorknob in my left. In one motion I threw the door violently inward. The dog—a huge black beast, and utterly ferocious to look upon —recoiled reflexively, then gathered herself to spring at my throat.

I pointed the gun and fired.

Eighteen

The dart went right where I'd aimed it, taking Astrid in the left shoulder. Bouviers have a dense curly coat and there was no way to be sure the dart wouldn't get deflected en route, and for a moment I thought it had because she seemed unaffected by it.

Then the tranquilizer hit. Astrid was about halfway into her spring, forepaws off the ground, when all at once her eyes glazed over and her jaw went slack. Her paws worked in the air like the feet of the coyote in the Roadrunner cartoons when he runs off a cliff and tries to keep going. Astrid couldn't keep going. She settled back down again, her spring unsprung, and then she wobbled like a child in high heels, and finally she uttered a sort of whimpery sound and pitched over onto her side.

How do you check a dog's pulse? I actually tried, fumbling around with what I don't suppose you call a wrist when you're dealing with a dog, but I gave that up because I didn't know what I was doing, and what difference did it make, anyway? If she was alive all I could do was let her sleep it off, and if she was dead there was nothing anybody could do for her, and my own course of action was the same in either case.

And I didn't have all the time in the world, either.

I raced up the stairs. The bedroom was in good order now, I saw. Sheets of plywood had been secured over the broken skylight, and the pastoral landscape once again hung on the wall, hiding the safe. I took it from its hook, fluffy sheep and rose-cheeked shepherdess and all, and placed it on the bed.

I wasn't sure if I'd remember the safe's combination or not. I'd thought about it in the cab on the way over, trying to put all the numbers together in the proper sequence, but once I was up there with my fingers on the dial I took the problem away from my mind and entrusted it to my hands, and they remembered. I opened the safe as if its combination were written out for me.

Five minutes later—well, no more than ten, anyway—I was hanging Little Bo Peep back where she belonged. I did a couple of other things, and in the second-floor library I sat at a leather-topped kneehole desk and used a modern reproduction of an old brass telephone to call Narrowback Gallery. I gave a progress report and established that Colcannon had not called since Carolyn sent him to Madison and Seventy-ninth.

I asked how long Astrid was likely to remain unconscious. "I don't know," Carolyn admitted. "I bought the dart gun because it's supposed to be a good thing to have around, but I never used the thing. I didn't think you would need it, to tell you the truth. She's always a perfect lady when I give her a bath. She never even growls."

"Well, she was ready to kill a few minutes ago."

"It's a territorial thing, I guess. If she hadn't been on her own turf she'd have been gentle."

"If she hadn't been on her own turf," I said, "we wouldn't have met. I just wish I knew how much time I've got."

"Maybe you'd better not take any longer than you have to.

164

That stuff works longer on a small dog than a large one, and Astrid's no Yorkie."

"No kidding. She's the Hound of the goddamn Baskervilles, is what she is."

"Well, get done as quickly as you can, Bern. If you have to use a second dart it might kill her. Or it might not work at all, or I don't know what."

I hung up and made another phone call, this one to the pay phone at Squires coffee shop at Madison and Seventy-ninth. I asked the woman who answered if she would summon Mr. Madison to the phone, and explained she'd be likely to find him at one of the rear booths. A moment later he said, "Well? Where are you?"

"I'm at a pay phone in a coffee shop, same as you. Let's not use names, shall we? I don't like to talk over an open line."

"Then why didn't you come here in person?"

"Because I'm afraid of you," I said. "I don't know who you are and you seem to know a lot about me. For all I know you're a violent person. I don't want to take the chance."

"Do you have the coin?"

"I picked it up this morning. I don't have it with me now because I'm not willing to run the risk. It's in a safe place and I can pick it up on short notice. I'm calling you now because I think we should set a price."

"Name your price."

"What's it worth to you?"

"No, that's not how we'll work it, sir." He seemed quite confident now, as if bargaining was something with which he had some reassuring familiarity. "Set your price, and make it your best price, and I shall say yes or no to it."

"Fifty thousand dollars."

"No."

"No?"

"According to the newspapers, a woman was killed when the coin was taken."

"Ah, but nobody knows that the coin was connected with her death. Except you and me, that is. And her husband, of course."

"Quite. I can pay you ten thousand dollars. I never argue price, sir."

"Neither do I. I'll take twenty."

"Impossible."

Twelve thousand was the price we settled on. He probably would have gone higher, but my skill in negotiation was diminished by my knowledge that I didn't have a coin to sell, so why knock myself out? We agreed on the price, and he agreed to bring the money in old out-of-sequence bills, nothing larger than a hundred. I don't know where he was going to find the money, since the banks were closed and there was no cash in the safe, but maybe he had a friend he could go to or had cash stashed around the house. I hadn't searched the place in the fine-comb style I'd employed at Abel's apartment, nor did I intend to, not with the formidable Astrid stretched out downstairs in uncertain sleep.

"We can make the exchange tomorrow," I said. "A friend of mine died this past week and there's going to be a memorial service for him over in Brooklyn. Nobody knows me there and I don't suppose anybody'll know you either, though I can't say that for sure because I don't know you myself. Do you have a big following in Cobble Hill?"

"I'm afraid not."

"Then we're in good shape. The service is at the Church of the Redeemer at two-thirty tomorrow afternoon. That's on Henry Street between Congress and Amity, and now you know as much about getting there as I do. I'll have the coin in an envelope, and if you could have the money the same way, we could make the exchange. I suppose there must be a bathroom, churches generally have bathrooms, and we can go there together and make sure it's the right coin and the money's all present and accounted for."

"I don't see why we have to meet in Brooklyn."

"Because I have to be there anyway, and because I won't pick up the coin until I'm on my way to the service, and because I want to make the swap in a public place, but not so public that there are likely to be police looking on. If you don't want to do it, I'm inclined to say the hell with it and put the coin in a gum machine, because this million-dollar coin has dropped in value to twelve grand and that's not all the money in the world to me, to be frank about it. So we'll do it my way or we won't do it at all, and maybe that's a better idea anyway, come to think of it."

I let him cajole me out of my snit. I didn't require too much in the way of cajolery. It wasn't that deep a snit. Then I said, "Wait a minute, how will we recognize each other? We've never met."

"I'll know you. I've seen your picture."

He'd done better than that. He'd seen me face to face, through a pane of presumably one-way glass. And I'd seen him the same way, although he didn't know it. I went along with the charade, saying I didn't look all that much like my picture and I wanted to be able to recognize him, too, so why didn't we both wear red carnations? He agreed, and I advised him to pick up his flower that evening, because it might be difficult finding a florist open on Sunday.

And through all this chatter I kept listening for Astrid's footfall on the stairs. At any moment she might come awake, anxious to demonstrate how attack dogs got their name.

"Tomorrow, then," he said. "At two-thirty. I'll be glad when this is over, Mr.— I almost said your name."

"Don't worry about it."

"As I said, I'll be glad when this is over."

He wasn't the only one.

I made sure the gun was armed with a little plastic dart, hurried downstairs with it and had a quick look at Astrid. She lay as I'd left her, sprawled on her side, and now I could see her chest heave with heavy breathing. While I stood there she made a small mewling sound and her forepaws twitched.

The dart that had done the job lay alongside her. I retrieved it, dropped it into my attaché case.

I went upstairs and used the phone again. I had a lot of people I wanted to call, but I limited myself to dialing three numbers, all of them long distance. None of the calls lasted very long. After the third one I went back downstairs to find the big black dog almost awake but not quite able to get up on her feet. She turned woebegone ill-focused eyes on me, and it was difficult to regard her as a threat. She looked incapable of a hostile thought, let alone of tearing one's throat out. But I forced myself to remember her bark, and the way she'd coiled herself to spring.

I hoped she'd be her old alert self by the time her master returned.

I let myself out, locked up after myself. If anyone watched me I was unaware of it. I walked through the garden, still wondering if there were fish in the pond, and I searched the flower beds in vain for carnations, red or otherwise. I could have suggested that he wear a tulip.

Why, I wondered, had I bothered with that carnation business? All in the interests of verisimilitude, I suppose, but it could add an unnecessary complication, because now I had to remember to pick one up before the stores closed. Which ordinarily wouldn't have been such a chore, but it was one of a long list of things to do, and I had less than twenty-four hours to get them all done.

Which left me no time to squander in gardens. I hurried through the tunnel, looked left and right and straight ahead, opened the gate and let myself out.

So many things to do . . .

Nineteen

"I dunno, Bern. What it sounds like to me is you're settin' up somethin' complicated."

"Isn't that what you wanted? You know I didn't have anything to do with either the Colcannon burglary or the murder of Abel Crowe, but you kept sniffing around, trying to stir something up."

"You're in both of those things up to your eyes, Bern. I just don't know about this, that's all."

It was Ray Kirschmann's day off and he was wearing brown gabardine slacks and a print sport shirt. The pants were baggy in the seat and too tight at the waist, and the shirt was one of those Korean imports in light green with dark-green stitching on the collar and pockets. I really wish he'd take his wife along when he buys clothes.

I said, "What's to know, Ray? I'm giving you a chance to be a hero, make a couple of good busts, clear a few old cases and put a few dollars in your pocket. What else do you expect to do? Slay the dragon and screw the king's daughter?"

"I don't care about dragons, Bern."

"You wouldn't like a princess much. One pea under the mattress keeps them bitching all night."

"Yeah, I remember the story. Tell me again about the dollars I'm gonna put in my pocket."

"There's a man who's willing to pay a reward for the recovery of his property."

"What man?"

"You'll meet him tomorrow."

"What property?"

"You'll find that out tomorrow, too."

"How am I gonna recover it? That's somethin' else I'll find out tomorrow. This is soundin' like those old radio programs. 'Tune in tomorrow an' see what happens to Jack Armstrong, the all-American boy.' Remember Jack Armstrong, Bern? Whatever did happen to him?"

"He's doing short time at Attica."

"Jesus, what a thought. How much of a reward are we talkin' about?"

"Ten grand."

He nodded, sucked his teeth. "But it's not offered officially," he said. "The guy could welsh."

"If it's not official it doesn't have to be reported, either. No taxes to pay. No splits with anybody higher up in the department."

His face took on a crafty look, and greed sparkled in his eyes. Spinoza may not have had a good word to say for avarice, but how would the wheels turn without it?

"The hell," he said. "We'll see how it goes."

"Have you got that list?"

He nodded, drew a folded sheet of paper from the pocket of the green sport shirt. "These here are burglaries committed in the past two years with an M.O. like the Colcannon job—forced entry and the place left like the burglars brought a cyclone with 'em. And it's the area you said—Manhattan south of Forty-second Street, west of Fifth Avenue and north

170

of Fourteenth Street. Computers are wonderful. You just say what you want and you got it."

"You wouldn't believe how comforting it is to know the police have these tools at their command."

"I can imagine. You're not the first person to figure Rabbit Margate might have done this kinda thing before, you know. They been questionin' him left and right. Not goin' back two years, and not just the neighborhood you picked, but they been askin' him a question or two."

"Are they getting anywhere?"

"He's still bein' Humphrey Bogart."

"Yesterday you said he was Jimmy Cagney."

"Same difference."

"You'll bring him tomorrow?"

"It's irregular. If he got loose and took a powder I'd have a little trouble explainin' it. I guess I could take a chance."

"And you don't know who was working with him?"

"Not yet. He'll talk sooner or later."

"Then I'll see you tomorrow," I said, and went over the time and place with him again.

"Anythin' I should bring? Besides Rabbit?"

"Your gun."

"I'm never without it."

"Not even in the shower? Let me think. Handcuffs, Ray. Bring plenty of handcuffs."

"Like I'm gonna arrest the whole Jesse James gang or somethin'. Well, you generally delivered in the past, Bern, so I'll play along. Anythin' else I can do for you in the meantime? Want a lift anywhere? Anythin' I can do to grease the skids for you a little?"

I thought it over, then resisted temptation. "No," I said. "I can manage."

I found Marilyn Margate at Hair Apparent. She was combing out a hard-faced woman with a headful of unconvincing auburn hair. "He admits he sleeps with his wife," the woman was saying, "but he insists he never enjoys it, that it's just a sense of duty. But my experience is they always tell you that, so how do you know what to believe?"

"I know just where you're coming from," Marilyn said. "Believe me, I know."

When she had a minute I drew her aside and gave her a slip of paper with the time and place of Abel's service. "It's important for you to show up," I said. "And bring Harlan Reese."

"Harlan? You think he went back and killed Wanda? That doesn't sound like Harlan."

"Just bring him."

"I don't know. He's not even leaving his room. And he was talking about splitting for the Coast or something before the cops get onto him. I don't think he's gonna want to chase out to Brooklyn for some old guy's funeral."

"Get him to come anyway. Your brother'll be there."

"Rabbit's gonna be there? You mean they let him out?"

"They'll release him for the service. I arranged it."

"You—" Her eyes were wide, her expression respectful. "That's some kind of arranging," she said. "That's more than the lawyer could do. They wouldn't set bail for him. Wait'll I tell his lawyer."

"Don't tell his lawyer anything."

"Oh. All right."

"Just show up tomorrow with Harlan."

"If Rabbit's gonna be there, I'll get there. And I'll bring Harlan."

I called Narrowback Gallery and Denise answered. "I hope you're free tomorrow," I said. "I'd like you to come to a funeral in Brooklyn."

"I'll wear a smock and a smile. You want to talk to your partner in crime?"

"Please."

She put Carolyn on and I said things were going well,

albeit hectically. "I have to get into Abel's building," I said, "and I decided not to ask Ray for help because I didn't want him to know what I was up to. Any bright ideas?"

"I guess it's a little late for another doctor's appointment."

"It's Saturday and it's close to dinnertime. That does make it tricky."

"If there's anything I can do—"

"I can't think of anything. I'll probably be tied up most of the night, assuming I find a way in. I thought maybe I'd drop over to your place after I'm done."

"Well, I sort of have a date, Bern."

"Oh. Well, I'll see you tomorrow at Abel's service. You'd better take down the address, or did I give it to you earlier?" I gave it to her again and she wrote it down. Then I asked her to put Denise on.

"Carolyn has the address for the service tomorrow. That's assuming that the two of you are speaking."

"You assume a lot."

"Uh-huh. What I wanted to say is I've got a batch of things to do tonight but I'll be done sooner or later, and I thought maybe I could drop over."

"Oh."

"Because I'd like to see you."

"Tonight's a bad night, Bernie."

"Oh. Well, I guess I'll see you tomorrow in Brooklyn."

"I guess so. Okay to bring Gore and Truman?"

"They're already on my list."

A machine answered Murray Feinsinger's telephone, inviting me to leave my name and number or call back at nine Monday morning if I wanted to speak to the doctor. I hung up without leaving a message and read through the listing of Feinsingers in the Manhattan directory until I found a listing for one Dorothy Feinsinger at the same address and dialed the number. Murray himself answered it.

I said, "Dr. Feinsinger? My name's Bernard Rhodenbarr,

173

I was in to see you yesterday afternoon. About my feet."

"That's why most people come to see me, Mr. Rhodenbarr. My office is closed for the day, and—"

"I don't know if you remember me. I had Morton's Foot, and you're going to be making orthotics for me."

"They're not ready yet, of course. It takes a couple of weeks."

"Yes, I understand that. But I gave you a deposit, just a small deposit really, and—"

"I'm afraid I've already sent the order in, Mr. Rhodenbarr. Is there a problem?"

"No problem at all," I said, "but I had a sudden cash windfall this afternoon, as a matter of fact I had a good day at the track, see, and I wanted to pay you the balance due before I blow it on necessities. And I'm in the neighborhood, so I thought maybe I could come up and pay you what I owe you, I guess it comes to two hundred and seventy dollars because I paid a thirty-dollar deposit, and—"

"That's very considerate of you, Mr. Rhodenbarr. Why don't you stop in Monday?"

"Well, Monday's a hard day for me, and for all I know the money might be gone by then. It wouldn't take a minute if I could just come up and pay you and—"

"I can't really take money outside of business hours," he said. "I'm at my apartment. My office is across the hall and it's closed, and I'd have to open up and make out a receipt for you and enter the cash in my books, and I'd rather not do all that."

"A receipt's not important to me. I could just pop up, pay you the cash, and off I'd go."

There was a pause. By now he must have been certain he was dealing with a lunatic, and why should he want to invite a lunatic upstairs? There should have been a way to get to see him, but I had evidently blown it, and everything I said now was only going to make it worse.

"Well, I'll see you Monday," I said. "I hope I still have

174

the money by then. Maybe I'll put it in my shoe in the meantime."

Brooklyn Information had a listing for a J. L. Garland on Cheever Place. The operator had no better idea than I if that was in Cobble Hill, but she said the exchange sounded about right, so I dialed it and got a chap with a sort of reedy voice. I asked to speak to Jessica and she came to the phone.

"This is Bernie Rhodenbarr," I told her. "I'll be there tomorrow, and I just wanted to confirm the time and place. Two-thirty at the Church of the Redeemer, is that right?"

"That's correct."

"Good. There are a couple of people I'd like you to call, if you would. To ask them to come. Neighbors of your grand-father's."

"I already posted a notice in the lobby. But you can call anyone yourself if you think it's advisable."

"I've already invited several people, as a matter of fact. I'd appreciate it if you'd make these particular calls, though. Could you write this down?"

She said she could and I gave her names and numbers and told her what to say. While I was doing this it occurred to me that she might have access to Abel's apartment. I wasn't quite sure I wanted to visit the place in her company, but it looked to be better than not going at all.

So I asked her if she'd been up to the place since the murder, and she hadn't. "I don't have keys," she said, "and the doorman said the police had left strict instructions not to admit anyone. I don't know that they'd let me up anyway. Why?"

"No reason," I said. "I just wondered. You'll make those calls?"

"Right away."

A few minutes after eight I presented myself at Abel Crowe's building. The doorman was a stranger to me, even as I presume I was to him. He looked as assertive as Astrid the Bouvier and I hoped I wouldn't have to take him out with a tranquilizer dart in the shoulder.

I had the dart pistol along, albeit not at hand. It was in my attaché case, along with burglar's tools, a fresh pair of palmless rubber gloves, and my wide-track Pumas. I was wearing black wingtips for a change, heavy and leather-soled and not particularly comfortable, but a better match than Weejuns or Pumas for my funereal three-button suit and the somber tie with the muted stripe.

"Reverend Rhodenbarr for Mrs. Pomerance in 11-J," I said. "She's expecting me."

Twenty

"He had European manners," Mrs. Pomerance said. "Always a smile and a kind word. The heat of summer bothered him, and sometimes you could tell his feet hurt by the way he walked, but you would never hear a complaint out of him. Not like some others I could mention."

I wrote "real gent" and "never complained" in my little notebook and glanced up to catch Mrs. Pomerance sneaking a peek at me. She didn't know how she knew me and it was driving her crazy. Since I was clearly the sincere Brooklyn clergyman Jessica Garland had called her about, the obliging chap gathering material for Abel Crowe's eulogy, it hadn't occurred to her that I might also be the Stettiner boy who'd shared an elevator with her a day earlier. But if I was Reverend Rhodenbarr of Cobble Hill, why did I look familiar?

We sat on plump upholstered chairs in her overfurnished little apartment, surrounded by bright-eyed photographs of her grandchildren and a positive glut of bisque figurines, and for twenty minutes or so she alternately spoke well of the dead and ill of the living, doing a good job of dishing the building's other inhabitants. She lived alone, did Mrs. Pomerance; her beloved Moe was cutting velvet in that great sweatshop in the sky.

It was about eight-thirty when I turned down a second cup of coffee and got up from my chair. "You've been very helpful," I told her, truthfully enough. "I'll look forward to seeing you at the service tomorrow."

She walked me to the door, assuring me she wouldn't miss it. "I'll be interested to see if you use anything I told you," she said. "No, you have to turn the top lock, too. That's right. You want to know something? You remind me of somebody."

"The Stettiner boy?"

"You know him?"

I shook my head. "But I'm told there's a resemblance."

She closed the door after me and locked up. I walked down the hall, picked Abel's spring lock and let myself into his apartment. It was as I'd left it, but darker, of course, since no daylight was streaming through his windows.

I turned some lights on. I wouldn't have done this ordinarily, not without drawing drapes first, but the closest buildings across the way were also across the river, so who was going to see me?

I did a little basic snooping, but nothing like the full-scale search I'd given the place the day before. I went through the bedroom closet, looking at this and at that, and I paid a second visit to the cigar humidor. Then I browsed the bookshelves, looking not for stashed loot but simply for something to read.

What I would have liked was my Robert B. Parker novel. I would have enjoyed finding out what was going on with old Spenser, who was evidently capable of jogging without orthotics and lifting weights without acquiring a hernia. But light fiction was harder to find in that place than a 1913 V-Nickel, and any number of books which might have been interesting were less so because of my inability to read German, French or Latin.

I wound up reading Schopenhauer's *Studies in Pessimism,* which was not at all what I'd had in mind. The book itself was a cheap reading copy, a well-thumbed Modern Library edition, and either Abel himself or a previous owner had done a fair amount of underlining, along with the odd exclamation point in the margin when something struck his fancy.

"If a man sets out to hate all the miserable creatures he meets," I read, *"he will not have much energy left for anything else; whereas he can despise them, one and all, with the greatest ease."*

I rather liked that, but a little Schopenhauer does go a long way. I thought about playing a little music, decided that having turned on some lights was as dangerously as I cared to live for the time being.

Some of that ancient Armagnac would have gone nicely. I had a little milk instead, and somewhere between ten and eleven I turned off the lights in the living room and went into the bedroom and got undressed.

His bed was neatly made. I suppose he must have made it up himself upon arising on the last morning of his life. I set the bedside alarm for two-thirty, crawled under the covers, switched off the lamp and went to sleep.

The alarm cut right into a dream. I don't recall what the dream was about, but it very likely concerned illegal entry of one sort or another because my mind promptly incorporated the wail of the clock into the dream, where it became a burglar alarm. I did a lot of fumbling for the off-switch in the dream before I tore myself free of it and fumbled for the actual clock, which had just about run down of its own accord by the time I got my hands on it.

Terrific. I sat for a few minutes in the dark, listening carefully, hoping no one would take undue note of the alarm. I don't suppose anybody even heard it. Those old buildings are pretty well soundproofed. I certainly didn't hear anything, and after a bit I switched on the lamp and got up and dressed.

This time, though, I put on the Pumas instead of the black wingtips. And I put my gloves on.

I let myself out of Abel's apartment, pushing the latch button so that the spring lock wouldn't engage when I closed the door. I walked down the hallway past the elevator to the stairwell, and I walked down seven flights of stairs and made my way to 4-B.

No light showed beneath the door. No sound was audible within. There was only one lock on the door, and you could have taken it to the circus and sold it as cotton candy. I let myself in.

Ten minutes later I let myself out and locked the door behind me. I climbed up seven flights of stairs, let myself back into Abel's apartment by the simple expedient of turning the knob, closed and locked the door, took off my trusty Pumas and everything else, set the bedside alarm for seven, and got back into bed.

And couldn't sleep at first. I got up, found a robe in the closet, put it on. It dawned on me that I hadn't eaten enough all day to sustain a canary, so I went into the kitchen and knocked off the rest of the Black Forest cake and finished the quart of milk. Then I went back to bed and slept.

I was up before the alarm. I had a quick shower, found a safety razor and shaved with it. It was strange, living in his apartment, as if I'd slipped into the very life my old friend had lately given up, but I didn't let myself dwell on it. I made a cup of instant coffee, drank it, and got dressed. I put on the dress shoes again and packed the Pumas in the attaché case, along with another of the books I'd been browsing earlier.

Neither the elevator operator nor the doorman gave me a second glance. They had never seen me before, but I was leaving at a civilized hour of the morning, and even in a stuffy old co-op on Riverside Drive there are surely some tenants

180

of either gender who are apt to have the occasional stranger spending the occasional night, and leaving under his or her own power by light of dawn.

Hair Apparent was on Ninth Avenue a few doors north of Twenty-fourth Street, next to a restaurant called Chelsea Commons. It was closed, of course, with a folding steel gate similar to the one I had at Barnegat Books. A padlock secured the gate across the doorway. I stood there in full view of passers-by and used a piece of spring steel to tease the lock until it opened.

Nobody paid any attention. It was broad daylight—and shaping up to be a beautiful day in the bargain. And I was well-dressed and obviously respectable, and to anyone watching I'd have looked as though I were using not a lock-pick but a perfectly legitimate key. Nothing to it, really.

Not much more to the business of unlocking the door. It took a little longer but it wasn't terribly tricky.

Then I opened the door and the burglar alarm went off.

Well, these things happen, in life as in dreams. I'd noted the alarm when I'd dropped in on Marilyn Margate the previous afternoon, and I'd looked around long enough to spot the cut-out switch on the wall near the first chair. I walked into the shop, proceeded directly to the cut-out switch, and silenced the shrill wailing.

No harm done. The neighbors were very likely used to that sort of thing. Business proprietors set off their own alarms all the time when they open up. It's when an alarm goes off in the middle of the night, or sounds for a long time unattended, that people reach for the phone and dial 911. Otherwise they assume it's all business as usual.

Anyway, what sort of idiot would burglarize a beauty shop?

I spent better than half an hour burglarizing this one. When I left, everything was as I had found it, with the sole exception of the burglar alarm, which I didn't reset for fear of setting it off again on my way out. I left the money in the register—just a few rolls of change and a dozen singles. And I left the gun Marilyn had pointed at me; she'd returned it to her employer's drawer, and that's where I let it remain.

I wiped the surfaces I was likely to have touched—rubber gloves didn't go well with my outfit. And I locked up after myself, and drew the window gates shut, and fastened the padlock.

Carolyn's number didn't answer. I started to call Denise, then changed my mind. I walked east on Twenty-third Street and read the plaques on the Chelsea Hotel, which boasted not of pediatricians and podiatrists in residence but writers who'd lived there in the past—Thomas Wolfe, Dylan Thomas. At Seventh Avenue I turned right and walked on downtown. Now and then I would pass a church, the worshipers all fresh-faced and spruced up as if in celebration of the season. A beautiful morning, I told myself. You couldn't ask for a finer day to bury Abel Crowe.

Of course, I reminded myself, we wouldn't actually bury him today. That would have to wait. But, if the service went as I hoped it would, perhaps we could lay my old friend to rest—his spirit if not his body. I had spent a night in his apartment, the apartment in which he'd been struck down and killed, and I couldn't say that I felt the presence of a restless spirit, an unquiet ghost. Then again, I'm not much at feeling presences. Someone who's more sensitive to that sort of thing might have felt Abel's shade close at hand in that living room, pacing the oriental carpet, crying out for vengeance. Just because I'm not aware of those things doesn't mean they don't exist.

I walked down below Fourteenth Street and had a big breakfast at a coffee shop in the Village—eggs, bacon, orange juice, toasted bran muffin, plenty of coffee. I picked up the Sunday *Times,* threw away all those sections nobody reads, and took the rest to Washington Square. There I sat on a bench, ignored all the obliging young men who offered to sell me every mood-altering chemical known to modern man, and read the paper while watching people and pigeons and the occasional ditsy gray squirrel. Kids climbed on the monkey bars. Young mothers pushed prams. Youths flung frisbees to and fro. Bums panhandled. Drunks staggered. Chess players advanced pawns while kibitzers shook their heads and clucked their tongues. People walked dogs, who ignored the signs and fouled the footpath. Drug dealers hawked their wares, as did the sellers of hot dogs, ice cream, Italian ices, helium-filled balloons, and organic snacks. I spotted my favorite vendor, a black man who sells large fuzzy yellow ducks with bright orange bills. They are the silliest damned things I have ever seen, and people evidently buy them, and I have never been able to figure out why.

I walked from the park to the subway, and by one-thirty I was in Cobble Hill and twenty minutes later I was at the Church of the Redeemer. I met Jessica Garland and the young man she lived with. His name was Clay Merriman, and he turned out to be a lanky fellow, all knees and elbows and a toothy smile. I told them both what I had in mind. He had a little trouble following me, but Jessica grasped it right away. Well, why not? She was Abel's granddaughter, wasn't she?

We looked over the room where the service was to take place. I told her where to seat people, assuming they didn't grab seats on their own. Then I left her and Clay to greet the guests as they arrived, biding my time in a room down the hall that looked to be the minister's study. The door was locked, but you can imagine the kind of lock they put on a minister's study.

At two-thirty the canned organ music started. By now the guests should have arrived, but stragglers will straggle, so the service itself was not going to start for another ten minutes. I waited out those ten minutes in the minister's study, doing a little pacing of the sort one probably does when rehearsing a sermon.

Then it was time. I took two books from my attaché case, refastened its clasps and left it in a corner of the room. I made my way down the corridor and entered the larger room where a fair crowd of people had assembled. I walked down the side aisle, mounted a two-foot platform, and took my place at the lectern.

I looked at all those people and took a deep breath.

Twenty-one

"Good afternoon," I said. "My name is Bernard Rhodenbarr. I'm here, as we all are, because of my friendship for Abel Crowe. Our friend and neighbor was struck down in his own home this past week, and we have assembled here to pay final tribute to his memory."

I looked over my audience. There were a great many unfamiliar faces in the crowd, and I guessed the older ones belonged to Abel's neighbors from Riverside Drive while the younger ones were Cobble Hill friends of Jessica's. Among them were quite a few people I recognized. I spotted Mrs. Pomerance in the second row, and my hearty podiatrist was one row behind her. Over to the left Ray Kirschmann sat beside a skinny young man with a lot of forehead and not much chin, and it didn't take a great leap of logic to guess I was looking at George Edward Margate. His ears were no longer than anybody else's, and his nose didn't exactly twitch, but it wasn't hard to see why they called him Rabbit.

His sister Marilyn was in the first row all the way over on the right. She was dressed quite sedately in a black skirt and dark-gray sweater, but all the same she looked like a whore in church. The man sitting beside her, a round-faced lumpish lout, had to be Harlan Reese.

Denise and Carolyn were sitting together all the way at the back. Carolyn was wearing her blazer. Denise had a sweater on, but I couldn't see whether she was wearing pants or a skirt. No smock, though, and no smile.

As chief mourner, Jessica Garland sat front row center, with Clay Merriman on her left. A pity we hadn't all met before this unhappy occasion, I thought. Abel could have had us all over of an evening, Clay and Jessica and Carolyn and I, and we could have fattened up on pastry while he regaled us with stories of Europe between the wars. But, oddly, he'd never mentioned a granddaughter.

Three men in dark suits sat together at the right of the third row. The one closest to the center was tall and balding, with a long nose and very thin lips. Beside him sat the oldest of the trio, a gentleman about sixty with wide shoulders, snow-white hair and a white mustache. The third man, seated on the aisle, was a small and slightly built fellow with a button nose and thick eyeglasses.

I had never seen them before but I was fairly certain I knew who they were. I paused long enough to meet the eyes of the white-haired man in the middle, and while his face did not change its stern expression he gave a short but distinct nod.

At the opposite end of the second row sat another man I recognized. Oval face, clipped mustache, slate-gray hair, little mouth and nose—I'd seen him before, of course, but Jessica had known where to put him because Herbert Franklin Colcannon had obligingly worn a carnation in his lapel.

I winced when I saw it. Somehow with all the running around I'd done I hadn't remembered to get to a florist before they closed. I suppose I could have let myself into a shuttered flower shop that very morning, but the act seemed disproportionately risky.

Anyway, I'd just introduced myself to the company. So Colcannon knew who I was.

"We're told our good friend made his living as a receiver of stolen property," I began. "I, however, knew him in another capacity—as a student of philosophy. The writings of Spinoza were particularly precious to Abel Crowe, and I would like to read a brief passage or two as a memorial to him."

I read from the leatherbound copy we'd given to Abel, the copy I'd retrieved Friday and had subsequently packed in my attaché case the following night. I read a couple short selections from the section entitled "On the Origin and Nature of the Emotions." It was dry stuff, and my audience did not look terribly attentive.

I closed Spinoza, placed the book on the lectern, and opened the other volume I'd brought along, one I'd selected last night from Abel's shelves.

"This is a book of Abel's," I said. "Selections from the writing of Thomas Hobbes. Here's a passage he underlined from *Philosophical Rudiments concerning Government and Society:* 'The cause of mutual fear consists partly in the natural equality of men, partly in their mutual will of hurting; whence it comes to pass that we can neither expect from others nor promise to ourselves the least security. For if we look on men full-grown, and consider how brittle the frame of our human body is, which perishing, all its strength, vigor and wisdom itself perisheth with it; and how easy a matter it is even for the weakest man to kill the strongest; there is no reason why any man trusting to his own strength should conceive himself made by nature above others. They are equals who can do equal things one against the other; but they who can do the greatest thing, namely kill, can do equal things.' "

I skipped to another marked passage. "This is from *Leviathan,*" I said. " 'In the nature of man, we find three principal causes of quarrels. First, competition; second, diffidence; thirdly, glory. The first maketh man invade for gain, the second for safety, and the third for reputation.' "

I placed Hobbes with Spinoza. "Abel Crowe was killed for gain," I announced. "The person who killed him is right here. In this room."

It was not without effect. The whole crowd seemed to draw breath at once. I fixed my eyes for the moment on Carolyn and Denise. They'd known what was coming but my announcement had gotten to them just the same, and they'd drawn a little closer together as if the drama of the moment had obscured their loathing for one another.

"Abel was murdered for a nickel," I went on. "People are killed every day for trifling sums, but this particular nickel was no trifle. It was worth something like a quarter of a million dollars." Another collective gasp from the crowd. "Tuesday night Abel came into possession of that coin. Twelve hours later he was dead."

I went on to tell them a little about the history of the five legendary 1913 V-Nickels. "One of these nickels wound up in the safe of a man who lived in a carriage house in Chelsea. The man and his wife had left town and weren't expected back until the following day. Tuesday evening, while they were gone, a pair of burglars broke through the skylight and ransacked the carriage house."

"We didn't take no nickel!" Heads swiveled and eyes stared at Rabbit Margate. "We never took no nickel," he said again, "and we never opened no safe. We found the safe, sure, but we couldn't punch it or peel it or nothing. I don't know shit about no nickel."

"No."

"And we didn't kill nobody. We didn't hurt nothing. Wasn't nobody home when we went in, and we went out again before nobody came home. I don't know shit about no murders and no nickels."

He slumped in his seat. Ray Kirschmann turned to whisper something to him, and Rabbit's shoulders sagged in dejection. I don't know what Ray said, probably pointed out Rabbit had just admitted the burglary in front of God and everybody.

"That's true," I said. "The first burglars, Rabbit Margate and Harlan Reese"—and didn't Harlan look startled to hear his name spoken aloud—"contented themselves with burglary and vandalism. Not long after they left, a second burglary took place. This burglar, a considerably more sophisticated and accomplished individual than Margate and Reese, went directly to the wall safe, opened it, and removed a pair of earrings, a valuable wristwatch, and the 1913 nickel. He took them directly to Abel's apartment, where he left them on consignment."

No point, really, in mentioning we'd obtained some cash for the watch and earrings. No need to tell these people every last detail.

"While the second burglar was delivering the safe's contents to Abel Crowe, the nickel's owner and his wife were returning to their home. They'd had a change of plans that none of the burglars had any reason to be aware of, and so they walked in on a house that looked like Rome after the Goths sacked it. They also walked in on another burglary in progress, and this third burglary was the charm. The man and woman were knocked out and tied up, and when the man regained consciousness and worked free of his bonds he discovered that his wife was dead."

I looked at Colcannon. He returned my glance, his face quite expressionless. I had the feeling he'd have preferred to be almost anywhere else, and I don't suppose he figured he was going to have the chance to buy his coin back, not this afternoon. He looked like a man who wanted to walk out of a bad movie but had to stay to find out what happened next.

"The nickel's owner called the police, of course. He was given the opportunity to look at the perpetrator of the second burglary but couldn't identify him. Subsequently he did make a positive identification of one of the participants in the first burglary."

"That was a frame," Rabbit Margate called out. "He never saw me. That was a setup."

"Let's just call it a mistake," I suggested. "The gentleman was under a lot of stress. He'd lost his wife, his house had been cruelly looted, and a coin worth a fortune was missing.

"And here's something interesting," I said, glancing again at Colcannon. "He never mentioned the coin to the police. He never said a word about it. You have to report losses to the police in order to make an insurance claim, but that didn't mean anything in this instance because the coin wasn't insured. And it wasn't insured for a very good reason. The gentleman didn't have title to it."

"This has gone far enough." It was Colcannon who spoke, and he managed to surprise me, not to mention the rest of the crowd. He got to his feet and glared at me. "I don't know how I let myself be gulled into coming here. I never knew the late Mr. Crowe. I was brought here on a false pretext. I never reported the loss of a 1913 V-Nickel and never carried insurance coverage on such a coin for a much better reason than the one you've advanced. I never had such a coin in my possession."

"I almost believed that for a while myself," I admitted. "Oh, I knew you had one, but I thought it might be a counterfeit. I ran a check on the five V-Nickels to find out which one you bought, and it turned out that they were all accounted for. Four were in museum collections and the fifth was privately owned, and the private specimen was lightly circulated and easily distinguishable from the others, and certainly not the specimen I took from your safe."

Another collective gasp—I'd gone and blown my anonymity, and now all and sundry knew who the perpetrator of the Second Burglary was. Ah, well. These things happen.

"But I had a good close look at that coin," I went on, "and I couldn't believe it was a counterfeit. So I did a little more checking and I invited some museum people to take a close look at their coins, and three of the four told me their coins looked just fine, thank you.

"The fourth museum had a counterfeit in the case."

I looked at the three men in dark suits. The one seated on the aisle, the little button-nosed guy with the thick glasses, was Milo Hracec, and he recognized his cue. "It was not a bad counterfeit," he said. "It was made from a proof 1903 nickel. The zero was removed and a one soldered in place. It was good work, and no one glancing into our display case would be likely to think twice about it, but you could never sell it to anyone as genuine."

The white-haired man cleared his throat. "I'm Gordon Ruslander," he announced. "When Mr. Hracec reported his discovery to me I went immediately to see for myself. He's right—the coin's not a bad counterfeit, but neither is it terribly deceptive at close glance. It's certainly not the coin I received when I traded a painting to the Baltimore Historical Society. That was a genuine specimen. I knew they wouldn't palm off a counterfeit on me, but as a matter of course I had it X-rayed anyway, and it was authentic. The coin that had been substituted for it didn't have to be X-rayed. It was visibly fraudulent."

"What did you do after you'd seen the coin?"

"I went to my curator's home and confronted him," he said. The man on Ruslander's other side, the balding chap with the long nose, seemed to shrink in his seat. "I knew Howard Pitterman had been having his troubles," Ruslander went on. "He went through a difficult divorce and had some investment reverses. I didn't realize just how hard his circumstances had been or I would certainly have offered help." He frowned. "Instead he took matters into his own hands a couple of months ago. He substituted a counterfeit for the 1913 nickel, then sold off our most important rarity for a fraction of its value."

"I got twenty thousand dollars for it," Howard Pitterman

said, his voice trembling. "I must have been insane."

"I don't know who that man is," Colcannon said, "but I've never seen him before in my life."

"If that's the man who bought the coin," Pitterman said, "he didn't buy it from me. I sold it to a dealer in Philadelphia, a man with a shady reputation. Maybe he sold it to this Mr. Colcannon, or maybe it went through another pair of hands first. I wouldn't know. I could give you the name of that dealer, although I'd rather not, but I don't think he'd admit to anything, and I can't prove he bought the coin from me." His voice broke. "I'd like to help," he said, "but I don't see that there's anything I can do."

"I'll say it again," Colcannon said. "I don't know any disreputable coin dealers in Philadelphia. I scarcely know any reputable ones. I know Mr. Ruslander by reputation, of course, as the founder of the Gallery of American and International Numismatics as well as proprietor of the Liberty Bell Mint, but I've never met him or his employees."

"Then why did you call Samuel Wilkes yesterday?"

"I never heard of Samuel Wilkes."

"He has an office near Rittenhouse Square," I said, "and he deals in coins and medals, and shady's the word for him. You called him yesterday at his home and left your name, and you called his office, and you also put in a call to the Gallery of American and International Numismatics. You made those calls from your home telephone, and since they're long distance there'll be a record of them."

There would be a record, all right. Colcannon was staring at me, trying to figure out how there would be a record of calls he had never made. Any minute now he'd recall that he'd been lured away from his house and hustled off to Madison and Seventy-ninth, and he might even figure out that he'd had company in his absence, but right now he seemed content to deny the whole thing.

"I never heard of this Wilkes," he said, "and I never called him, and I certainly didn't call the gallery."

"What's it matter anyway, Bern?" It was Ray Kirsch-mann, and I wasn't sure how much of this he was following. "If Crowe got killed for this nickel, all right, that makes sense, but who cares how the nickel got into the safe? Crowe got killed after it got outta the safe."

"Ah," I said. "What's significant is that nobody knew it was in the safe in the first place. Except for the Third Burglar."

"The *who?*"

"Rabbit Margate and Harlan Reese didn't know about the nickel," I went on. "All they knew was that the Colcannons were going to be out of town overnight. They knew that because Wanda Colcannon got her hair done at a beauty shop called Hair Apparent, where Rabbit's sister Marilyn was one of the operators. And she was quite an operator. Among her customers in the past year and a half, eight of them got burglarized while they were out of town on vaca-tion. All eight of those burglaries had the same modus ope-randi. A crude break-in, a completely messy burglary, and a pattern of vandalism that was almost deliberate in nature. Marilyn just kept her ears open when her customers talked about going out of town, and she passed on the information to her brother, and that was all it took. What good does it do to stop the milk and mail and leave the lights on a timer if the sweet young thing who does your hair has a burglar for a brother?"

I avoided looking in Marilyn's direction while I said all this. Now I caught Carolyn's eye. "Wanda used to stop in my bookstore when she brought her dog for grooming at a place down the street." Might as well keep Carolyn out of it. "The last time I saw her, she happened to mention she was taking the animal out of town to be bred. So, like Rabbit and Harlan, I had inside information. I knew the Colcannons would be away overnight, and they knew the same thing.

"But the Third Burglar knew no such thing. The Third Burglar was waiting for the Colcannons to come home. Ever since I realized there was a third burglar involved, I've tended to think of him in capital letters, like the Third Murderer in *Macbeth*. Shakespearean scholars have a lot of fun with the Third Murderer, you know. Shakespeare didn't give him all that much to say, so the evidence is pretty sketchy, but one school of thought holds that the Third Murderer was actually Macbeth himself."

A hush went over the room. It was, all things considered, one of your better hushes.

"That was a clue from my subconscious," I said, "but it took me a while to put it together. No one with inside information could have been the Third Burglar, because then he'd have known not to expect the Colcannons that night. And for someone to have dropped in through the skylight just by chance and then hanging around to commit homicide—well, it seemed to be stretching coincidence pretty thin. But my subconscious was trying to tell me something, and ultimately I managed to piece it together. Whether or not Shakespeare meant the Third Murderer to be Macbeth, the Third Burglar was Herbert Franklin Colcannon."

He was on his feet. "You're crazy," he said. "You're a raving maniac. Are you trying to say I staged a burglary of my own house? That I stole this nonexistent coin from myself?"

"No."

"Then—"

"There was no third burglary," I said. "Rabbit and Harlan stole everything they could find, and I took the three items from your safe, and that's as much burglary as you had that night. There was no third burglary and there was no Third Burglar, and there was nobody hanging around to hit you over the head and tie you up. You killed your own wife."

Twenty-two

For a moment no one said anything. Then Colcannon told them that I was out of my mind. "Why are we listening to him?" he demanded. "This man is a self-confessed burglar and we're sitting here while he hands around accusations of larceny and homicide. I don't know about the rest of you, but I've had enough of this. I'm leaving."

"You'll miss the refreshments if you leave now."

His nostrils flared and he stepped away from his seat. Then a hand took him by the elbow and he spun around to meet the eyes of Ray Kirschmann.

"Easy," Ray told him. "Whyn't we have a listen to what Bern there has to say? Maybe he'll come up with somethin' interestin'."

"Take your hand off me," Colcannon barked. His bark was less reminiscent of a Bouvier than, say, a mini-poodle. "Who do you think you are?"

"I think I'm a cop," Ray said agreeably, "and Bern thinks you're a murderer, and when he has thoughts along those lines they tend to pan out. Long as he's got the ball, let's just see where he runs with it."

And where would that be? "Mr. Colcannon's right about one thing," I said. "I'm a burglar. More accurately, I'm a bookseller who's trying to break himself of the habit of burglary. But one thing I'm not is a policeman, and it's going to be the job of the police to put together a case against Colcannon for murdering his wife.

"But maybe I can tell them where to look. His finances wouldn't be a bad place to start. The Colcannons lived well and they owned a lot of valuable things, but the rich get into financial difficulties the same as the rest of us.

"One thing that made me suspicious was the emptiness of that wall safe when I opened it. One watch, one pair of earrings, one rare coin, plus a handful of papers—people who own wall safes generally utilize them more, especially people with attack dogs who believe their premises are impregnable. I made a few telephone calls yesterday, and I learned that Mr. Colcannon has been selling off some of the coins he's bought in recent years."

"That proves nothing," Colcannon said. "One's interest changes. One sells one article to buy another."

"Maybe, but I don't think so. I think you took a couple of major gambles recently—your safe contains some stock certificates that represent securities you've taken a heavy loss on. And I think you paid a damn sight more for the 1913 V-Nickel than the twenty grand Mr. Pitterman received for it. You probably couldn't afford that nickel when it came available, but you had to have it because you're an avaricious man, and unless Spinoza was off base, avarice is a species of madness, and not an endangered one, either.

"You bought the nickel, shelled out for it at a time when you were trying to raise cash to meet your other obligations. Then you took your dog to be bred—another damned expense, although it would pay off when Astrid had her pups —and you rushed back to New York rather than stay overnight in Pennsylvania, and maybe you and your wife had an argument at the theater or during dinner afterward. That's something the police can find out if they do a little legwork.

"It hardly matters. The two of you walked into your house to find the unmistakable evidence of a burglary. Maybe you'd been planning on selling various valuables that they'd walked off with. Maybe you were underinsured. You probably didn't ever think to raise the insurance coverage on your silver, hardly anybody does, and now the nice windfall you'd had during the sharp rise in silver was wiped out by thieves in the night.

"And maybe your wife made some smartass remark right about then, and maybe it was the last straw. Or did it just remind you that one of the few things remaining in your wall safe was an insurance policy on both your lives? If either of you died, the other collected half a million dollars. And there's a double indemnity clause for accidental death, and the companies consider murder an accident, although it's generally undertaken on purpose, which is a contradiction, don't you think? Maybe the first time you hit her was out of rage, and then the possibility of gain suggested itself to you. Maybe you took one look at the looted rooms of your house and saw instantly that the burglary would make a good smoke screen for murder. We probably won't know the answer to that one until you confess, and you probably *will* confess, Mr. Colcannon, because amateurs generally do. And you're an amateur. You're an absolute pro at avarice, sir, but you're an amateur at homicide."

I meant he'd most likely confess at the police station, not in front of the lot of us. But a shadow passed over his face right about then and I decided to shut up for a minute and give him room. Or rope, if you like.

His lip quivered. Then a muscle worked in his temple. "I didn't mean to kill her," he said.

I looked at Ray and Ray looked at me, and a smile blossomed on Ray's lips.

"I hit her once. It was an accident, really. She was railing at me, nagging me. She could be such a shrew. She'd married me for my money, of course. That was no secret. But now that money was tight—" He sighed. "I swung at her. I could never have done that if the dog had been around. The bitch would have taken my arm off. I swung and she fell and she must have hit her head on something when she reached the floor."

It was nice embroidery. I'd seen those pictures, and the woman had been systematically beaten to death, but let Colcannon put the best face on it for the time being. This was the opening wedge. Later on they'd crack him like a coconut.

"Then I tried to find her pulse and she was dead," he went on, "and I thought that my life was over, too, and then I thought, well, let the burglars take the blame for this one. So I tied her up and I struck myself over the head, it was hard to make myself do that hard enough to inflict damage but I steeled myself, and then after I'd set the stage I called the police. I thought they'd question me and break me down, but they took one look around and knew the house had been looted by burglars, and that evidently satisfied them."

Ray rolled his eyes at the ceiling. Some members of the department, I suspected, were going to hear about this one.

"But I never killed Abel Crowe!" Colcannon was bristling suddenly with righteous indignation. "That's what all this was supposed to be about, isn't it? The murder of a receiver of stolen goods? I never met Abel Crowe, I never even *heard* of Abel Crowe, and I certainly didn't kill him."

"No," I agreed. "You didn't."

"I didn't know he had my coin. I thought *you* had my coin."

"So you did."

"I thought you still had it. That's why I came here today in the first place, God damn it to hell. So how can you accuse me of killing Crowe?"

"I can't."

"But—"

I sent my eyes on a tour of my audience. I had their

attention, all right. I looked straight at the murderer and saw nothing there but the same rapt interest that was evident on all their faces. .

"I think you would have killed Abel," I told Colcannon, "if you had thought it would get you the coin back. For all I know you were planning to kill me this afternoon rather than pay me the twelve thousand dollars for the coin. But you didn't know he had the coin, and there was no way you could know."

"Unless Abel told him," Carolyn piped up. "Maybe Abel tried to sell the coin back to him."

I shook my head. "Not at that stage," I said. "He might have tried to work a deal with the insurance company, after the loss was reported. But it was too early for Abel to know that the loss wasn't covered by insurance, and far too early for him to think about selling the coin back to its presumptive owner.

"My first thought was that Abel had invited a prospective buyer to view the coin, and that he'd sufficiently misjudged the man's character to get murdered for his troubles. But was that the first thing Abel would do?"

I shook my head. "It wasn't," I answered myself. "Abel had just received a coin with a six-figure price tag. It had come from the hands of a thief who in turn had taken it from the house of a man who was not known to have possession of it. Before Abel did anything with the coin he had to determine whether or not it was genuine. Even though he could approach certainty by examining it closely, one doesn't take chances. Mr. Ruslander obtained the coin from a reputable museum, but even so he took the normal precaution of having it X-rayed to determine its authenticity, and Abel would do no less when dealing with a coin of doubtful provenance.

"Abel said at the time that such a determination was his first order of business. 'At a more favorable hour,' he said, he could verify the coin's legitimacy without leaving the building. I took this to mean that he could have an expert numismatist drop by to look at the coin and authenticate it, but experts of that sort don't habitually make house calls in the middle of the night.

"But that wasn't what he meant at all.

"He meant that there was someone in his building who could provide verification of the coin's bona fides. I thought there might be a numismatic expert in residence, and then I stopped to think about it and realized that Abel wouldn't want an expert to know that he had the coin. The 1913 V-Nickel's too rare and too celebrated, and the real experts in the coin field are highly ethical men who would balk at authenticating a stolen coin and being expected to keep quiet about it.

"No, what Abel required was not an opinion. He wanted an X-ray."

I scanned my audience. The murderer remained quite expressionless, so much so that I almost doubted my conclusion. But not really. I glanced at Carolyn and saw her nodding intently. She had it figured now.

"Where do you go for an X-ray? A lab? A hospital emergency room? A radiologist? You couldn't manage that without leaving Abel's building. A dentist? There's a dentist in the building, a Dr. Grieg. I believe he specializes in root canal work."

"He does," Mrs. Pomerance confirmed. "He doesn't hurt you, either, but he charges a fortune."

"They all charge a fortune," someone else said. "Grieg's no worse than the rest of them."

"Abel had false teeth," I said, "so I doubt he'd have needed Dr. Grieg's services, reasonable or otherwise. He might have become friendly with the man regardless and have used his X-ray equipment for examining rare coins and jewelry, but he wasn't a patient, and Abel doesn't seem to have developed intimate relationships with his neighbors.

"Anyway, Abel had a professional relationship with some-

"I did," he said, then caught himself and shook his head violently. "I did not take any keys," he said, trying to cover. "I did not kill him, I did not take the coin, I did not take any jewelry, and I most certainly did not take any keys."

"You certainly didn't get rid of them. They're in the drawer with the earrings and the watch." And they were, too. Not the set he'd taken with him, but who was to know that?

Well, *he* knew it. "You've framed me," he said. "You planted those things."

"Did I plant the nickel, too?"

"You won't find the nickel in my possession."

"Are you sure of that? When the police search the place thoroughly? When they turn it upside down and know what they're looking for? Are you absolutely certain they won't find it? Think it over."

He thought about it, and I guess I was convincing, and evidently he had a higher opinion of the cops' ability to find a needle in a haystack than I did, because before anybody knew what was happening he'd pushed his chair back and shoved past the woman seated beside him and was on his way to the door.

Ray had his gun out almost immediately, but he was in the wrong position and there were too many people between him and Feinsinger, all of them on their feet and making noise. I could have let him go—how far was he going to run, orthotics or no?

Instead I reached under my jacket and got my gun. I yelled for him to stop, and when he didn't I tranquilized the son of a bitch.

Twenty-three

"What we want is Irish coffee," Carolyn said, "and where we want to go for it is McBell's."

McBell's is in the Village, on Sixth Avenue a couple of blocks below Eighth Street, and we went there by cab. It's not terribly hard to find a Brooklyn cabbie willing to go to Manhattan, although it can be quite a trick convincing a Manhattan cabbie to go to Brooklyn, which just proves once again that we live in an inequitable universe, and when was that ever news?

By this time the tumult and the shouting had died and the captives and the kings had departed, the kings in this case being Ray Kirschmann and a couple of stalwarts from the local precinct whom he'd called to help him with the captives. There were enough of the latter to go around—Murray Feinsinger, Herbert Franklin Colcannon, George Edward "Rabbit" Margate, and, lest we forget, Marilyn Margate and Harlan Reese.

Jessica and Clay invited us back to their place, along with most of the crowd from the service, but I said we'd take a rain check. Nor did we spend much time talking with the three-man delegation from Philadelphia. It looked as though no charges would be pressed against Howard Pitterman, who was evidently a good curator when he wasn't rustling his employer's cattle. I had the feeling Milo Hracec was in for a bonus, and arrangements had already been made for Ray Kirschmann to put a ten-thousand-dollar reward in his pocket the day the coin found its way back to its rightful owner. Normal procedure would call for the nickel to be impounded as evidence, but normal procedure can sometimes be short-circuited when the right cop is properly motivated, and Gordon Ruslander had agreed to provide the proper motivation.

The cabbie took us over the Brooklyn Bridge, and it was a glorious view on a glorious Sunday. I sat in the middle, Denise on my right and Carolyn on my left, and thought how fortunate a man I was. I'd solved two murders, one of them a friend's. I'd admitted to burglary in front of a roomful of people and didn't have to worry about being charged with it. And I was riding into Manhattan with my girlfriend on one side of me and my best buddy on the other, and they'd even left off sniping at each other, and who could ask for anything more?

Carolyn was right about the Irish coffee. It was what we wanted, all right, and it was as it ought to be, the coffee rich and dark and sweet with brown sugar, the Irish whiskey generously supplied, and the whole topped not with some glop out of a shaving-cream dispenser but real hand-whipped heavy cream. We had one round, and then we had a second round, and I started making noises about eventually rounding off the day with a celebratory dinner, all three of us, unless of course somebody had other plans, in which case—

"Shit," Denise said. We were sitting, all three of us, around a tiny table that had room for our three stemmed glasses and one big ashtray, and she'd almost filled the ashtray already, smoking one Virginia Slim after another. She ground one out now and pushed her chair back. "I can't take any more of this," she said.

"What's the matter?"

"I'm coming unglued, that's all. You two talk, huh? I'm going home so my kid doesn't forget what I look like. The two of you can kick it around, and then you'll come over to my place later, all right?"

"I guess so," I said.

But she wasn't talking to me. She was talking to Carolyn, who hesitated, then gave a quick nod.

"Well," Denise said. She grabbed up her purse, drew a breath, then put a palm on the table for support and leaned over to kiss Carolyn lightly on the mouth. Then, cheeks scarlet, she turned and strode out of the place.

For a few minutes nobody said anything. Then Carolyn managed to catch the waiter's eye and ordered a martini. I thought about having one myself but didn't really feel like it. I still had half of my second Irish coffee in front of me and I didn't much feel like finishing that, either.

Carolyn said, "Couple of things, Bern. How'd you know Marilyn Margate set up all those burglaries?"

"I figured she knew Mrs. Colcannon. When she turned up with a gun in her purse and accused me of murder, she called the woman Wanda. I figured they were friends, but what kind of friend gets her brother to knock off a friend's house? And it couldn't have been coincidence that Rabbit and Harlan found their way to Eighteenth Street, any more than it was coincidence they picked a time when nobody was home.

"Then when I dropped in at Hair Apparent I overheard a woman talking about something personal, and I realized women tell their hairdressers everything, and I got a list of similar burglaries committed in the immediate area of the beauty parlor."

"And you found some of the names in their appointment book when you went there this morning. Bern? Wasn't that doing it the hard way? Couldn't you have just called the burglary victims and asked where they got their hair done?"

"I thought of that. But that wouldn't prove Wanda got her hair done at Hair Apparent. Besides, if I couldn't find any of the other names in the appointment book, I could always write them in myself."

"Falsify evidence, you mean."

"I think of it more as supplying evidence than falsifying it. For another thing, I could have wound up spending hours on the phone without reaching anybody. People tend to go out on Saturday night. But maybe the most important reason, aside from the fact that I'm a burglar and it's natural for a burglar to take a burglaristic approach to problems, is that I wanted to see about the gun."

"The gun?"

"The one Marilyn brought to my apartment. I was relieved to find it in a drawer. She'd said she had put it back, but if I didn't find it I was going to assume it was still in her purse, and that would have meant tipping off Ray so that she didn't get a chance to pull it when I exposed her role in the burglaries."

"I see."

"Uh, Carolyn—"

"Shit. You probably want to talk about Denise."

"I don't know that I *want* to. But I think we have to. Don't we?"

"Double shit. Yeah, I guess we probably do." She finished her martini, looked around in vain for the waiter, then gave up and put her glass down. "Well, I'll be damned if I know how it happened, Bern. God knows I didn't plan it."

"You didn't even like her."

"Like her? I couldn't stand her."

"And she wasn't crazy about you."

"She despised me. Detested me. Thought of me as a dwarf who smelled like a wet dog."

"And you thought she was bony and gawky."

"Well, I was wrong, wasn't I?"

"How did it—"

"I don't *know,* Bern." The waiter sailed by and she caught him by the hem of his jacket and pressed her empty glass into his hand. "It's an emergency," she told him, and to me she said, "I swear I don't know how it happened. I guess there must have been an attraction all along and our hostility was a cover-up for it."

"Best cover-up since Watergate."

"Just about. The thing is I feel awful about it and so does Denise. We started off yesterday forcing ourselves to tolerate each other, and there was something in the air, and we both sensed it, and I decided to deny it, because I knew I didn't want to make a pass. In the first place she was your girlfriend and in the second place she wasn't gay."

"So?"

"So she kept getting flirtier and flirtier, and you know me, Bern, I can resist anything but temptation. She wound up making the pass, and—"

"Denise made the pass?"

"Yeah."

"I never suspected she was gay."

"I don't think she is. I think she's straight enough to own a goddamn poodle, if you want to know, but right now she wants to go on going to bed with me, and I figure what I'll do is take it a day at a time and see where it goes. I don't think it's the love affair of the century, and if it's going to fuck up our relationship, Bern, then what I figure is the hell with her. There's women all over the place, but where am I gonna find another best friend?"

"It's okay, Carolyn."

"It's not okay. It's crazy."

"Don't worry about it. Denise and I weren't the love affair of the century, either. I called her the other day primarily because I figured I might need an alibi. You don't have to tell her that, but it's true."

"She already knows. She said so herself as a way of justifying our going to bed together."

"Well, what the hell."

"You're not upset?"

"I don't know what I am exactly. Confused, mainly. You know the story about the guy whose wife dies and he's all broken up at the funeral, and his best friend takes him aside and tells him how he'll get over it?"

"It sounds familiar. Keep going."

"Well, the best friend says that he'll get over it, the pain and loss will fade, and after a few months he'll actually start dating again, and he'll find a woman he responds to, and he'll fall in love and go to bed with her and start building a new life. And the bereaved widower says, 'Yeah, sure, I know all that, but what am I going to do tonight?' "

"Oh."

"Somehow I think Marilyn Margate is out. Even if somebody posts bail for her, I have a feeling she wouldn't welcome me with open arms."

"Not now. How come you threw her to the wolves? You didn't have to, did you?"

"Well, it didn't hurt. Improved the case against Colcannon, tied up a few loose ends."

"I thought, you know, honor among thieves and all. She and Harlan and Rabbit are fellow burglars or something, so I didn't think you'd tip them to the cops."

"Fellow burglars? You saw what they did on Eighteenth Street."

"Yeah."

"They weren't burglars. They were barbarians. The best thing I could do for the profession of burglary was get them the hell out of it."

"I suppose." She sipped at her new martini. "She was pretty cheap-looking, anyway."

"True."

"She must have been really sluttish in that red and black outfit."

"You might say so."

"Still," she said thoughtfully, "I can see how she'd be very attractive to someone who liked the type."

"Uh-huh."

"I like the type, myself."

"So do I."

"Of course it's not the only type I like."

"Same here."

"Bernie? You're not mad at me? You don't hate me?"

"Of course not."

"We're still buddies?"

"You bet."

"We're still partners in crime? I'm still your henchperson?"

"Count on it."

"Then everything's okay."

"Yeah, everything's okay. 'But what am I gonna do tonight?' "

"Good question." She stood up. "Well, I know what I'm gonna do tonight."

"Yeah, I'll bet you do. Give my love to Denise."

After she left I thought about having another Irish coffee, or a martini, or any of a number of other things, but I didn't really want anything to drink. Some of Abel's ancient Armagnac might have tempted me but I didn't figure they'd have it in stock. I settled our tab, added a tip, and went for a walk.

I didn't consciously aim my feet at Washington Square but that's where they took me all the same. I bought a Good Humor, the special flavor of the month, something with a lot of goo on the outside and a fudgy chocolate core inside the ice cream. I decided it might give me one of Carolyn's sugar hangovers and I decided I didn't give a damn.

For one reason or another I kept bench-hopping, sitting in one place for a few minutes and then turning restless and scouting out another perch. I watched the dealers and the drunks and the junkies and the young mothers and the courting couples and the drug dealers and the three-card-monte con artists and the purveyors of one thing or another, and I watched the joggers relentlessly threading their way through the walkers as they made their endless counterclockwise circuits of the park, and I watched the children and wondered, not for the first time, where the hell they got their energy.

I was still restless. For a change I had more energy than the children and no place to direct it. I got up after a while and walked past the chess players to the corner of Fourth and MacDougal. I was wearing a suit and carrying an attaché case and my shoes were too wide and I had Morton's Foot, but what the hell.

I tucked the case under my arm and started jogging.

And that would be as good a place as any to leave it, except that Jessica Garland turned up at my store a few days later with the two books I'd read from at the service. She said she wasn't a student of moral philosophy herself, and would I like to have Spinoza and Hobbes in remembrance of Abel?

"I just hope I'll get something of his myself sooner or later," she said. "He doesn't seem to have left a will, and there's some question as to my ability to prove I'm his granddaughter. I have letters from him, or Mum has them back in England, but I don't know if they'll constitute proof, and meanwhile I expect the estate will be tied up for a long time. Until then there's no way for me to get into his apartment."

"Even if you inherit," I said, "it'll have been searched by professionals first. I don't suppose Abel had clear title to most of the things he owned. Your best hope is that they won't find everything. Between the cops and the IRS people they'll find a lot, but there are things they'll miss. I'd be surprised if they get the money in the telephone." She looked puzzled and I explained, and told her something about the other treasures tucked away here and there.

"They'll likely disappear before I see them," she said. "Stolen or not, I suspect they'll walk out of there, wouldn't you say?"

"Probably. Even if Abel bought them legitimately." Not everyone, after all, shared my reluctance to rob the dead. "Maybe the doorman would let you in. You could at least get the money out of the telephone."

"I tried to get in. It's a very strictly run building from a security standpoint." She frowned, and then her face turned thoughtful. "I wonder."

"You wonder what?"

"Do you suppose *you* could get in? I mean it is rather your line of country, isn't it? And I'd be more than willing to give you half of whatever you managed to salvage from the apartment. I've a feeling I'll never see any of it otherwise, between the police and the inland revenue and whatever bite the death duties take, or do you call them inheritance taxes over here? Half of something is considerably more than a hundred percent of nothing. Could you do it, do you suppose? It's not really stealing, is it?"

"It's an impossible building to get into," I said.

"I know."

"And I've already found two different ways in and used them both up. And that was before half the tenants knew me by face and name, not to mention occupation."

"I know," she said, looking downcast. "I don't suppose you'd want to have a go at it, then."

"I didn't say that."

"But if there's no way for you to get in—"

"There's always a way in," I said. "Always. There's always a way to pick a lock, and to get past a doorman, and to open a safe. If you're resourceful and determined, there's always a way."

212

Her eyes were huge. "You sound in the grip of passion," she said.

"Well, I, uh—"

"You're going to do it, aren't you?"

I tried to look as though I was thinking it over, but who was I kidding? "Yes," I said, "I guess I am."